A CHARMING GHOST

A Magical Cures Mystery

Book Eight

BY
TONYA KAPPES

TONYA KAPPES
WEEKLY NEWSLETTER

Want a behind-the-scenes journey of me as a writer?
The ups and downs, new deals, book sales, giveaways and more? I share it all!

As a special thank you for joining, you'll get an exclusive copy of my cross-over short story, *A CHARMING BLEND.* Go to Tonyakappes.com and click on subscribe in the upper right corner to join.

CHAPTER ONE

I wasn't just cold. I was bone-numbing, toe-curling, potion-freezing cold. And no amount of snuggling with Oscar, and I tried, was going to drive out the chill that had crept up into my soul. Deep into my soul.

I reached over and grazed Madame Torres, my crystal ball, with the pad of my finger. Her globe flashed red lightning bolts until it settled into a display that showed it was four-thirty in the morning. She wasn't about to show her face. My snarky crystal ball was not a morning person—I was sure it took hours for her to get all dolled up in her head turban and gobs of makeup she wore—and lightning bolts were her subtle way of telling me that she was not happy with the early morning wake-up call.

I glanced over at Oscar, my husband of two months. Only my white fairy-god cat was sitting between us with his eyes focused on me and his butt facing Oscar, which I was sure was on purpose.

My familiars, Mr. Prince Charming and Madame Torres, were still harboring hard feelings over my marriage to my best friend, Oscar Park. They were a little possessive of me.

"You too?" I asked and let out a heavy sigh.

He put a paw on my arm and I gave him a little scratch between his ears. White fur flew everywhere. He jerked away, turning toward Oscar. He jumped on Oscar's chest using it as a springboard off the bed and darted out the bedroom door.

"Ouch," Oscar groaned in a groggy voice and rubbed his chest before he turned on his right side and began to snore lightly.

The moonbeams dotted the walls of the bedroom through the window blinds giving me just enough light to see my handsome new husband. His black hair blended into the dark room but seeing his silhouette outlined by the moon made my insides bubble with happiness. Even after two months of marriage, I still wasn't used to the fact that I was finally Mrs. Oscar Park, though I kept my legal name of June Heal for business purposes.

I sighed when seeing Oscar slumber didn't ward off the soul freeze. I shivered. I glanced over to the closed blinds and wondered what kind of weather we were having. There was snow predicted and maybe that was the cold that had settled deep in my bones.

I loved how our village of Whispering Falls, Kentucky looked when it was blanketed in snow. I loved how it added a little coziness to my little homeopathic cure shop, A Charming Cure. I liked to think I helped people feel better in a natural kind of way. . .umm. . .maybe with a little help from my spiritual gift.

I'm blessed beyond belief with the spiritual gift of intuition, which helps me create the perfect cure for the customers who walk into my shop looking for the right homeopathic cure for them.

Some people might see me as a witch—a good one, mind you—but I liked to refer to myself as a spiritualist. It just sounds better. I was from the Good-Sider community of the witch world, meaning we only did magic for the good.

Meow, meow. Mr. Prince Charming stood at the bedroom door.

"I'm coming." I peeled back the covers and tiptoed out of the room.

There was a lot to do at the shop and a lot of generic potions to be made; lying in bed wide awake wasn't going to help get the shop ready for the town's second annual Winter Bazaar that was taking place in a couple of days.

Oscar didn't have to go into work until later in the day and he deserved to sleep in. He had been pulling double-duty as the sheriff of Whispering Falls and a deputy of Locust Grove, the town over, which was not a magical town like Whispering Falls.

Mr. Prince Charming's long tail happily danced in the air in front of me as I hurried down the hall to the combination kitchen and family room of my little cottage on the hill overlooking the village. I ran my hand along my orange couch on my way to push the button to my coffee maker. A good cup of hot magical beans was what I needed to get the chill out of my soul.

I looked out the window and smiled at the small flakes of snow. The wind rushed around with snow in its breath, blanketing the rooftops of all the small shops. The smell of freshly brewed coffee danced around my nose. I sucked in a deep breath, my eyes focused down the hill along Main Street where the gaslight carriage lights flickered between the holes in the pine needle wreaths that were hung for decoration.

Puffs of smoke curled into the air and danced in grey swirls in the moonlight.

I followed the swirls to the ground and watched as a lantern swung back and forth from Eloise Sandlewood's grasp.

She swung the chain to the right and keeping in the same time, she swung it to the left giving each shop a morning cleanse just as she did every morning by using her spiritual gift as an Incense Spiritualist.

Her long green velvet cloak dragged behind her with each deliberate step. The edges of her bright red hair peeked out from the hood, shielding her from the brisk wind and blowing snow.

Eloise was Oscar's aunt and now mine, though I had loved her long before she became family. She happened to have been my mother Darla's best friend during the small amount of time my mother had lived here. Darla was not a spiritualist and when my father had gotten killed in the line of duty, Darla and I moved to Locust Grove where she tried to raise me as a mortal. Oscar also grew up in Locust Grove across the street from us. I was in love with him since day one. Little did we realize we were destined to fall in love. Only he was a Dark-Sider Spiritualist which made it a little tricky for us to get married, but that was a whole other story.

It was all well and good until Darla had died and the spiritualists had come looking for me (and Oscar). Neither of us had any idea about our pasts nor of our powers.

I watched Eloise cleanse the village with loving memories of how she was able to help me understand where I had come from and share more about my mother.

Rowl. Mr. Prince Charming stood on his hind legs and planted his paws on the window. I leaned over a little more, getting a look at what he was staring at.

Eloise had stopped in front of Magical Moments, the flower shop, a little too long. Longer than usual. She was facing my little cottage on the hill.

Her emerald green eyes glowed, a red aura circled around them. It was as if she weren't present. Her red lips moved at warp speed and the smoke from the incense burner puffed like a freight train. She gripped the chain in her hand, swinging the chain higher and higher, clinking louder and louder, echoing throughout the mountainous town.

The coffee maker buzzed, making me jump and turn away from the trance Eloise had put me in. I sucked in a deep breath and straightened my shoulders. Mr. Prince Charming jumped off the counter. And I watched him as he circled my ankles doing his signature figure-eight move.

My eyes slid back up to the window and down the hill, but Eloise was gone. The backdrop of the mountains was filled with the purple dawn just beyond the horizon, leaving me with the sudden chill deep in my soul that had woken me from slumber.

CHAPTER TWO

"Good morning!" I called out to Arabella Paxton, owner of Magical Moments and a florist and spiritualist who can read people by the flowers they choose. I touched the ornamental gate that lead up to Magical Moments. The iron stems of the gate turned green like the stems on flowers and blossoms of every color appeared all over the gate, creating its own little garden.

A giggle escaped my lips.

"I'm never going to get used to that." I winked and pushed my way through, heading to the top of the steps where Arabella had just put her key into the door leading inside Magical Moments.

Every shop in Whispering Falls had an ornamental gate and front door that led you inside the magical shop. Every shop owner had a spiritual gift and Magical Moments was a perfect cover for Arabella to use her gifts.

"Isn't it just lovely against this dreary day?" Arabella turned to greet me. Strands of her long black hair brushed against her olive complexion, sticking to her high cheek bones from the damp snowfall. Her crystal blue eyes deepened when she smiled. "Seeing you so happy does make the dreariness go away." She motioned for me to follow her. "Come on in. I have a new flower for the season to show you."

The inside of Magical Moments was truly magical and made me a little envious. My shop, A Charming Cure, displayed my potions on the table and mounted wall displays. But Magical Moments was an altogether different experience.

The sound of the babbling brook that ran through the center of the store gurgled and chirped. Colorful flowers grew along each side of the creek bed along with greenery, making it full and lush. The tiered black display tables were filled with premade vases of arrangements, emitting the most exotic smells.

"Over here." She pointed to the claw-foot table in the corner. The purple vase was a staple in the center of the fancy table, but the flowers always changed.

I hurried alongside her and tucked a strand of my black hair behind my ear. I had let my hair grow out for my wedding and it was driving me nuts. I couldn't wait for my appointment with Chandra Shango from A Cleansing Spirit Spa to get it cut later today.

"This is a flower that never needs water." Arabella's eyes twinkled. Her face brightened with pride.

The flower was rather bland and one I wouldn't have chosen to purchase if I was in Magical Moments as a customer. There were four, dull, white, almost wilted looking petals jutting out from a brown center seed. They ended in sharp points. The stem was thorny and bright green.

"It's definitely strange," I said and watched as she snapped the flower open and held it over her mouth. A little stream of water trickled out of the green stem and into her mouth.

"It's full of nutritious water." She smacked her lips together.

"Wow." My mouth dropped. I had never seen anything like it.

Sure, Arabella could touch a flower and bring it back or I could make a potion to help the life of the flower, but this was a whole new level of magic.

"Right?" she asked. Her lips came together. Her smile sent a sparkle to her eyes. "Good too."

"And what would be the purpose of this?" I questioned trying to tap into my intuition to see if I could use it in a homeopathic cure.

"Not sure yet. But I figured if I told you, then your little mind would go to work and figure something out for someone." She winked and pulled a couple of them out from the vase. "I'm going to make you a fabulous arrangement for your shop."

"Oh, I'd love it. What is the name of it?" I asked.

"Blood Mercy," she said and lifted one up in the air. She twirled the stem in between her fingers and observed it from all sides. "It's a strange name for such a lovely flower."

I smiled and pictured the perfect place for the flowers. Right next to the register where my customers will ask about them.

"Say." Suddenly I remembered why I had stopped by in the first place. I followed her to the table where she kept her tools for the pruning and whatever else she needed to create the beautiful arrangements for her clients. "Is everything going okay?"

"Splendid. Why?" She plucked, snipped, and fixed the flowers in a gorgeous green vase with little bubble-like bumps all over it. The bland Blood Mercy flower really wasn't all that ugly once Arabella dressed it in an arrangement with other flowers.

"Nothing that makes you feel like you need extra protection or a bad omen feeling?" I asked. My finger grazed over the snipped pieces as I tried to play off the question with unconcerned attitude.

"Um." She put the last piece of baby's breath in the arrangement and placed her hands palm down on the table. Her head tilted. Her mouth cocked to the side as if she were thinking long and hard or pulling something out from the back of her brain. "Nope," she shook her head. "Should I be?" Her eyes narrowed.

"No!" The word rushed out of my mouth. "Oscar said there was an emergency village council meeting this afternoon and I wondered if you knew anything about it. He didn't know and since your father. . ." I referred to Gerald Regiula, village council member and The Gathering Grove Tea Shoppe owner, her father.

"He hasn't said a word." She cackled. "He hasn't had energy to talk. Baby Orin is still keeping them up at night."

I smiled thinking about cute baby Orin. He was the son of Gerald and Petunia Shrubwood, not to mention the cutest baby in Whispering Falls. Well, the only baby in Whispering Falls and all of us spoiled him rotten.

"Hmm." I tapped my finger to my temple. "I just might have to see what I can come up with for him."

"Gerald or Orin?" Arabella pushed the vase toward me.

"Both." My brows lifted and I carefully picked up the vase. "I can't thank you enough."

"You are so welcome." She walked from behind the table and I followed her to the door where she flipped the sign on her door to OPEN. "You already have a line."

Both of us looked out the door. I tucked the vase in my elbow and opened Magical Moment's door.

"Gosh, I lost track of time." I scurried down the steps.

"Good morning." I called to the customers in the line as I made my way past them, under the wisteria vine and up the steps to the front door of A Charming Cure.

I put the vase on the ground and reached in my bag to retrieve the skeleton key to open my shop door.

Meow. Mr. Prince Charming stood underneath the archway where the purple wisteria vine was still just as lively as it was in the summer. Something dropped from his mouth.

I bent down to pick it up. Between the pads of my finger and thumb was a small brass bell charm.

Panic rioted deep within me as my intuition rang.

CHAPTER THREE

"Really?" My voice rushed underneath my breath as I spat toward Mr. Prince Charming. I juggled the vase of flowers and my mind, which was difficult when I tried to flip the sign on the door to OPEN and flipped on the switch of the cauldron sitting on the table next to the door.

I rushed to the counter and put the vase down next to the register where I knew it would look perfect. It did. I threw my bag on my chair and took a look around the shop. Customers were coming in and dispersing in all directions.

Any minute Faith Mortimer from Wicked Good Bakery would be here to deliver my morning supply of hot apple cider from The Gathering Grove and the delicious June's Gems from Wicked Good Bakery for my customers to enjoy while wandering through the shop. It was a great marketing tool to keep them looking while getting a free snack to eat. June's Gems were pretty addicting and I loved it.

Mr. Prince Charming darted to the back of the room and jumped on top of the counter next to the cash register where he loved to sit and watch over the shop. His nose lifted to the flowers and he checked them out.

"Can't you for once let me have a moment's peace?" I asked him. I unhooked my cloak and swung it off my shoulders, hanging it on the coat tree next to the counter.

Rowl! He hissed and jumped down. The red skirt on the round table closest to the counter brushed the floor as he swept under it to find a safe place from my anger.

The customers were picking up bottles, opening them, smelling them, giving me time to take a closer look at the charm. It wasn't like the other silver charms Mr. Prince Charming had given me every other time I needed protection from something coming my way. This time the charm was brass. Definitely different.

I tucked it away in the front pocket of my jeans. I ran my hand over the charm bracelet clasped around my wrist and recalled all the other times Mr. Prince Charming had showed up and dropped off a charm.

The first time was on my tenth birthday. I'll never forget it. I had always wanted a cat and a charm bracelet. Darla would give me neither. She insisted that cats were dirty and charm bracelets were too expensive. I thought she'd given in when Mr. Prince Charming showed up on the front steps of our house in Locust Grove with a charm tied around his neck.

It wasn't until years later when I had found out Mr. Prince Charming had been sent by the Order of the Elders and the Whispering Falls village council to keep me protected since I didn't live in the protection of the village. Somehow they had figured out that I did have the spiritual powers of my father and not the mortal side of Darla.

Darla must've known something was up because she let me keep him. He turned out to be my fairy-god cat, protecting me by giving me the charms, but somehow I always got dragged into crazy situations where people ended up dead.

There was no time to worry about this now. I had a full day of work and potions to make. The Christmas bazaar was in a couple of days and I hadn't even taken out the decorations from the attic of the shop, much less decorate the window display that the village council had requested already be done.

There was just too much to do to worry about a little ole charm, I told myself to feel a little better.

I took my hand from my charm bracelet and ran it across the framed photo from my wedding where Oscar and I were grinning ear-to-ear, Aunt Helena next to me, and Eloise next to Oscar. It was all the family we had. I had the perfect spot I wanted to hang it in the shop. Right on the wall next to the only other framed photo that was of my mom and dad. The only photo I had of them together.

I grabbed the hammer from underneath the counter and a small tack. I centered the frame perfectly under my parents' photo. Careful not to smash my fingers, I slowly nailed the tack and hung the wedding photo. It was exactly the right spot.

"You-whoo! June!" The voice could be heard, but the person was not seen. "Excuse me. Excuse me." A little louder, and a little louder, and then finally, "Excuse me!"

The customers parted and Constance Karima waddled past them and up to the counter. Her beady green eyes focused on me. Her white hair set in tight curls around her head, her glasses pushed up on the bridge of her nose, and her blue house dress swooshed with each heavy step.

"I am fed up to here!" Constance hand flew up to her neck in a karate chopping motion. "I'm not kidding."

"I can see that." I bit my lips together trying not to smile. My teeth clenched, pinching my skin together in more pain that I wanted. But the wrath of Constance would be worse. "How can I help you?"

"I told you a couple of months ago that my sister was nuts. One-hundred percent crazy and I know you got a little taste of it at your wedding." Her right eyelid lowered, her left brow cocked. She searched my face for a reaction.

"No." Slowly I shook my head, denying anything that I did see. It was between me and Patience Karima, Constance's twin sister. Exact twin.

"I came to you before your wedding and asked for your help." She jabbed the counter with her finger. "Now I am demanding your help! Demanding!"

"Shhh." I came from behind the counter when I noticed she had gotten some of the customers' attention. "This is not to be discussed here. This is a matter of the spiritual world," I leaned over and whispered into her ear. "You and I both know that rule number one in the by-laws state that no other spiritualist can read the other unless given permission."

"I'm giving you permission." She drew her finger up to her chest. "I have a funeral taking place next week and you have to get down there today and fix her. She is talking to herself, giggling out of her mind, and playing with that stupid ostrich." She huffed a sigh and crossed her arms over her chest. "If you don't fix her crazy, I'll never get this funeral together in a week."

The twins owned Two Sisters and a Funeral. It was the only funeral home in Whispering Falls and since we didn't have a lot of people dying, the village council allowed other surrounding counties to use the funeral home as well. And I must admit that it probably didn't look good if one of the funeral directors was acting a little coo-coo.

"You know that you can't do that," I said, and she opened her mouth to protest, I put my hand up to stop her. "But," her mouth snapped shut. "If it makes you feel any better, I will go see her and talk to her."

"Well," she turned her chin to the side and then up in the air, "it might make me feel a little better."

I placed my hand on the side of her arm and gave her a little squeeze.

"Good." I nodded. "I'll see if I can get Faith to come in after she does her deliveries and watch over the shop for a few minutes. I'm not guaranteeing anything."

Even though Constance accepted what I had told her I would do, I could tell by her snapping eyes that she wasn't all that happy.

I sucked in a deep breath. The smell of money floated around my head, up my nose, and past my shoulders over to an older man in the corner of the shop near the front windows.

"If you'll excuse me. I have a customer who needs my help." I gave Constance one last pat before I walked around her and over to the gentleman.

He stood about my height, five-foot-eight, had a thin build and wore a pair of brown khakis, brown loafers, a blue overcoat. His blond hair was short on the sides and spiked in the front with a little gel to look stylish.

"Good morning." I smiled and noticed he was looking at the stress-free lotions I had recently sold in the Head To Toe Works Store in a national deal.

Ever since the product hit the shelves of the national chain, A Charming Cure's front door had almost become one of those revolving doors in those fancy hotels.

"That is Gentle June's and a little dab will do you." The product here in the store was much different than the one I had created for Head To Toe Works.

My homeopathic spiritual gift was much better in person. Take this guy, he was looking at the stress-free lotions, which obviously means he was stressed. About what? Family? Job? Fire? Who knew? But I did. The lingering smell of money around him, which his body was emitting, told me how he was stressed about money. When someone was stressed about money, it only made the situation worse.

Given the age that he looked, I was under the assumption his money issues were probably related to retirement or not having enough for retirement.

My job was to put a little extra something in the bottle to not let him stress so much, prioritize his life or his situation and let the money begin to flow back into his world. I'd help him by adding a little extra to his bottle of stress-free lotion using my cauldron hidden behind the counter. That was how the magic in my shop worked.

The Head To Toe Works bottles worked differently. I was obviously not able to go to everyone's home who had purchased the product, so I had to put the magic in the bottle. When the customer touched the bottle, the bottle created the magic inside combining with the lotion.

It's very hard to understand, but that was how magic worked. At least in my world.

"I feel a little weird coming in here." The customer glanced around. "I mean, it's all women," he whispered.

"So. Everyone gets stressed and most men wouldn't recognize it." I snapped my finger and pointed at him. "That is why you are going to have an advantage over all the men in your industry."

"I already do." His shoulders shrugged when he laughed. "There are a lot of secrets in my *industry*." His emphasis on industry caused my gut to knot and my pulse quicken. He smiled, softening his face. "I mean that in a good way."

"In that case." I plucked the lotion from his hands. "I've got just what you need. I'll be right back."

My mind reeled with what his job might be, but asking him would be plain nosy. I was the answer to his problem, otherwise he wouldn't be in my shop and my intuition wouldn't have gone off. I could help him, but it was up to him to carry out the application of the potion.

The other customers in the store were content and occupied with all the different cures around the shop so I had time to start the guy's special lotion for his money troubles.

My eyes slid down to the floor where Mr. Prince Charming's tail was sticking out from underneath the table skirt. I walked behind the counter and grabbed my bag off the stool before disappearing behind the partition where my cauldron was hidden from the world.

Behind me was a couple of shelves. One held different ingredients; things like bat eye lashes, fish scales, Antimony tartrate, arsenic trioxide and flecks of human skin. And the other shelf held many different sizes, shapes, and colors of potion bottles.

I flipped the cauldron switch and proceeded to run my finger down the shelf of ingredients. With the customer in mind and the smell of money, the perfect ingredients would appear.

"Bushmaster snake." The bag with bits of the snake glowed. Without question, I picked the cloth bag up and continued down the line. "Thujua occidentalis?" I questioned when the bottle of wart remover glowed. Down the line I went and reached the last ingredient. "Calendula officinalis?"

I gulped and picked it up placing it next to the other two near the cauldron. None of these ingredients made sense to me. The Bushmaster snake was mostly used in a wide range of issues, so that wasn't so shocking, but the thujua occidentalis and calendula officinalis were alarming.

Thujua occidentalis was mainly used in warts and chronic conditions, and calendula officinalis was used in healing wounds. None of these were used with stressful money issues.

I sucked in a deep breath and closed my eyes. The smell of money was even more fragrant as the air filled my lungs. There was no way my intuition was off. There was more to this man than I knew, but he was here for one thing and according to my gift, he needed help with money.

I shook off my doubt and grabbed the Bushmaster first. Carefully I pulled on the cloth bag's drawstrings and pinched a piece of the snake off, throwing it into the cauldron.

The cauldron glowed a deep green and immediately began to bubble. I used the ladle next to the cauldron to stir, staying in tune with my intuition. Next I added in the thujua occidentalis and watched the potion smoke and turn amber in color. The smell of cotton candy flew from the pot and caused me to jerk my head. The sugary treat made my mouth water even though I hadn't had any cotton candy since Darla had taken me and Oscar to a traveling carnival in Locust Grove when we were children.

"What on earth?" I gulped. Something was off.

"June! Where are you?" I heard Faith Mortimer call from inside the shop.

I peeked my head around the partition and saw Faith next to the door. She was filling the cauldron with the apple cider and strategically placing the order of June's Gems on the three-tier plate.

I glanced back at the cauldron and quickly stirred it. I ran my hands down my apron, tucked a strand of hair behind my ear and went to greet Faith.

"Here you go." She smiled sweetly at one of the customers who came to get a sample of the cider. "Do you like Ding Dongs?" The customer nodded. "Then you have to have a June's Gem." She handed the customer one of the chocolaty treats named after me. "You will love it."

My go-to stress relief wasn't my own concoction of ingredients; it was the delicious treat of the Ding Dong. When Faith and her sister, Raven, moved to Whispering Falls to open Wicked Good Bakery, Raven made her own take on the Ding Dong and named them after me, June's Gem.

I grabbed one and shoved it in my mouth.

"Umm. Stressed?" Faith pulled back. Her long blond hair was pulled up in a high pony. Her onyx eyes watched me intently.

"A little." My eyes slid over to the gentleman. Something wasn't right with him, but it wasn't my job to fix all his problems, just the ones my intuition clued in on. "But I'm sure it will all be fine." I smiled. "Thank you for bringing these by. Are you busy today?"

"Oh gosh, extremely. Raven has me running two trips to Locust Grove's Piggly Wiggly today." She pointed out the window to the car with the big plastic cupcake on top. The pink and light green Wicked Good Bakery logo was printed across the side panels of the car.

"If you get finished early, do you think you could come by here this afternoon and man the shop?" I asked.

Faith was the only one in our village who I trusted working in A Charming Cure. She'd done it so many times before and I kept her on my payroll for these just-in-case times. Patience Karima was one of those just-in-case times.

"I'd be happy too." Her mouth twisted. "Because I have yet to hear anything for the paper." She tapped her ears.

Faith's spiritual gift was Clairaudience. She was able to hear things beyond the natural sense of hearing. She clearly heard words from other spirits, guides or angels in some magical way. This made her perfect for the job as the Whispering Falls Gazette's editor, our local paper. Only the paper wasn't in paper form, it was through wind and only for spiritualists to hear.

"I wondered why I hadn't gotten the news today." Most days the Gazette was delivered to me as I walked down for work in the morning. She and her sister lived above the bakery in their own apartment.

"Yeah." She shook her head. "Nothing."

"Isn't that strange?" I asked and handed a cup of steamy apple cider to a customer who walked through the door. "Please enjoy." I smiled and stepped to the side to let them pass.

"Maybe a little strange, but it's winter and Christmas, which really isn't our big holiday, so maybe things are quiet." She shrugged. "I better get going. I'll be back this afternoon to help out."

"Thanks!" I waved her off and looked around the shop. Satisfied that everyone was okay, I walked back to the counter and disappeared behind the partition. The potion was moving in a wave-like way. I took the cork top off the thujua occidentalis, adding a couple of dashes to the cauldron and a couple sprinkles of the calendula officinalis. The potion swirled; the murky, viscous substance turned silver and smelled like money.

Satisfied, I turned around and ran my finger down the bottle shelf until the brown, masculine bottle glowed tan. The bottles picked their owner and even though my intuition had a little hiccup, everything was coming together for the client.

I flipped the cauldron off and held the brown bottle over the cauldron, letting the potion pour into the container. I cleaned up the bottle and quickly wrote the instructions on a piece of paper.

When I came from behind the partition, the man was standing near the counter looking at my wedding photo.

"Did you just recently get married?" he asked.

"How can you tell?" I wondered.

"Your hair looks the same." He was very observant. "Is that your mother?"

"Oh no." I pointed to Aunt Helena. "That is my aunt and this is my husband, Sheriff Oscar Park, and his Aunt Eloise."

"Where are their husbands?" he asked.

"Good grief." I joked, "No man is going to marry them." I rolled my eyes. "They are set in their ways if you know what I mean."

"Your husband is the sheriff?" He drew back. The lines in the corner of his eyes deepened. He had to be older than he looked. "Very cool."

"He is a good guy." I held the bottle out to him. He didn't take it immediately, he just stood in front of the photo and stared. I spoke, "These are the instructions. You just use a dab on your lips like lip balm. It's amazing. You are going to love it."

"Lip balm, huh?" His eyes narrowed when he looked at me as if he were studying me.

"Just as easy as that." I handed him the bottle.

"Thank you very much." He handed me the cash. Our fingers touched, sending a shock of energy between us. A hazy warning breezed past me.

He didn't seem to notice and took the bottle. I stayed a couple of steps behind him on his way out. I pulled back the curtain in the display window and peeked around it.

The man jogged down the steps, the snow not hindering him at all. There was a smile on his face and he nodded his head as other customers passed him on the way in.

Abruptly he stopped when he nearly knocked over Petunia Shrubwood as she was heading toward her shop, Glorybee Pet Shop.

She and he exchanged glances. Their eyes traded a string of confusion as if there was something between them. I watched as they brushed each other off and went on their separate ways.

CHAPTER FOUR

By the end of the morning, the bustling snow had given way to a lone flying flake here and there, leaving a lovely thin blanket of snow on the sidewalks. The carriage lights had a thick layer on the steeple and the wreaths Arabella had made to hang on the each one had a dusting on the greenery. It was like I was back in Locust Grove, getting ready to celebrate the holidays.

Everyone in Whispering Falls had been reluctant over the past couple of years to do the Holiday Bazaar, but the turnout was so great, so helping to boost the economy the village council had decided to do it again.

I didn't mind because I loved celebrating all things Christmas, and dragging the boxes labeled "Christmas decorations" down from the attic really did put a spring in my step.

I dragged the box with the Christmas tree and decorations to the front of the shop where the window display would go and headed back to the counter. I pulled Madame Torres out of my bag and looked around the shop one more time to make sure there were no customers around.

"Good afternoon." I tapped on the glass ball.

"I cannot believe you woke me up at the God awful hour of four in the morning." Madame Torres was such an exaggerator. Her head appeared in the globe. Her eyelids heavy with purple eye shadow. Her lips lined with red, she spoke, "A girl of my age has to have her beauty sleep."

"And just how old are you?" I maneuvered into unchartered territory. I had no idea how old she was. In fact, I'd never asked.

Mystic Lights was the first shop I had gone into when I first came to Whispering Falls. I had gone to see Isadora Solstice about opening a shop here after she'd found me in Locust Grove. When I walked into the light store, I had no idea I was a spiritualist and I was about to be informed of my heritage. Madame Torres glowed every time I had gotten near her. And to my knowledge, or so I was told, crystal balls and their owners are destined only for each other for life.

Unfortunately, Madame Torres can be a little snarky at times and I loved to threaten her by telling her I'd take her to a flea market for someone to buy as a paperweight because she and I both knew she wouldn't be able to show herself unless she belonged to me.

"You dare ask such a question?" Madame Torres turned her head. Her red turban pinned tightly to her head. Her red flaming hair poked out from underneath.

"I was going to say how fabulous you looked for your age," I teased.

"What on earth is on your head?" Madame Torres questioned, her voice snarled.

"You don't like it?" I asked her and smiled when a photo of me in a red Santa hat floated in her glittery globe. She glared. "Merry Christmas!" I chirped in an annoying happy voice just to aggravate her even more.

"But seriously, can you give me a little festive music while I get the decorations up?" I was ready to get into the festive mood, even if I had to make myself forget the little brass bell charm.

"If I must." She disappeared from the globe and replaced herself with a light blue background and lightly falling snow. She looked like a snow globe. "But don't think I'm happy about it. I hate the cold and I hate the mortal holidays. So. . .um. . .friendly," she groaned before she played "White Christmas".

I opened another box and took out the pre-lit tree, standing it on its built-in base. The branches folded open and out. It was lunchtime and The Gathering Grove and Wicked Good both had lines out the door from the tourists. It was a perfect time to get the tree up in the display window and work a little magic.

The bell above the door dinged, letting me know someone had come in. I crawled out from under the tree where I was separating the last of the branches to find Oscar standing in the doorway with a cup of coffee.

"My hero." I blinked rapidly and clapped my hands together.

"You are adorable in that hat. You did always love Christmas when we were little kids." Oscar's smile grew as his hand extended toward me to hand me the coffee cup. "I figured you were getting tired and could use a pick-me-up. You tossed and turned all night."

"I did?" I asked and gave him a kiss.

"You don't remember?" He looked at me curiously, which I might have thought was odd, but his devilishly handsome looks in his sheriff's uniform outweighed any thoughts I might have had about anything.

"No." I shook my head and took a sip of the coffee. "Mmmm." The extra jolt of pumpkin spice calmed my soul. "Perfect choice."

"I'm a little concerned about why you were so restless." He wasn't about to let it die and I wasn't about to tell him about the sudden chill I had had in bed. It would only upset him and he'd stick close by my side.

Not that I didn't love him right by my side, but I had things to do, like get the window display up and people to see, like Patience Karima.

"I'm fine," my voice rose an octave. "See," I pointed over to Madame Torres, "I even have festive music playing." I ran my hand down my jeans, feeling the charm I had completely forgotten about in my pocket.

"What?" Oscar's eyes narrowed.

"What? What?" I asked, placing both hands on the sides of the cup and turned to look at my tree.

"You looked funny." He took a step closer.

"I do have a Santa hat on." I teased.

"Seriously." Oscar wasn't buying my hat excuse. He was always good at reading me and my expressions no matter how much I tried to conceal them. "You have never had a good poker face and if something is going on in that cute little head of yours, I need to know."

I put my finger up to his lips to stop him.

"I've got to get this window display finished and since everyone seems to be having lunch, it's perfect timing." I put the cup down on the table where the apple cider cauldron was located and picked up some garland out of another box so I could hang it around the window.

"Yeah, okay." Oscar wasn't buying it, but if I could get him out of the shop, I'd get down to Bella's Baubles to get this little matter of the bell charm addressed and find out what exactly it meant on my way to see Patience.

I looked out the window when I heard a car pull up across the street. It was Faith pulling up the cupcake car in front of Wicked Good. If she came over here to work, Oscar would really be asking all sorts of questions.

"Maybe we should go ahead and take our honeymoon." Oscar grinned from ear-to-ear. His devilishly handsome good looks made my heart pound and toes curl. His blue eyes popped against his olive complexion and his black hair had just enough gel in it to muss up the longer length on top and to slick the close-cropped sides.

"Honeymoon," I whispered, wondering just when we were going to get time away from the hustle and bustle of our duties in Whispering Falls. "You have that meeting. We have the bazaar. You know you can't take off in Locust Grove with the all the extra work they have for you there."

During the holidays, normal towns like Locust Grove always saw a rise in crime. They had put Oscar on the schedule more than usual to help patrol the shopping centers. Not like Whispering Falls. If someone tried to take something from any of our shops, our intuition would go off like the siren on top of the Two Sisters and a Funeral's ambulance.

"I guess you are right." He reached out and pulled me close to him.

His chin rested perfectly on top of my head. He whispered, "But you promise me that we will get away after all this stuff dies down."

"Promise." I curled up on my toes and granted him a slow and thoughtful kiss. Something that would hold him over until we got home tonight.

"Then I better get going to the emergency village council meeting." His eyes didn't leave my face. "Are you sure you are okay?" I really tried not to smile or even give a hint that I was a tad bit worried or that something was not right. Satisfied, he said, "I'll see you at home tonight?"

"Right after my hair cut." I reminded him of my appointment after all the shops were closed and Chandra could fit me in.

"Keep the hat on." He winked and pulled me close. He wrapped me in his arms and gave me a kiss before he left. The cold air pushed in when he shut the door behind him.

I jerked the hat off my head and tossed it aside.

I put my hand in my pocket and pulled out the charm, placing it in my palm. I rubbed it with my finger and watched Oscar run across the street to the police station.

Mewl, mewl. Mr. Prince Charming stared at me. He sat next to the Christmas tree.

"So." I shrugged and put the charm back in my pocket.

The tree was one of those pre-lit, easy-peasy kinds. I plugged in the lights and was happy to see they all appeared to work. The memory of how I'd slip out the door and meet Oscar under his big oak tree to share a Ding Dong while Darla was fussing each year with the big ball of knotted lights brought a smile to my face.

Meow, Mr. Prince Charming swept his tail back and forth dragging the floor.

I stepped back to get a good look at the whole tree. Looking up, I noticed the branches were flattened and stuck together so I lifted up on my tippy toes and spread a couple of the tree branches near the top. "I didn't have to tell him anything yet."

Rowl! Mr. Prince Charming stood up on his hind legs and batted at the dangling charm bracelet from my wrist. He and Oscar might have a love-hate relationship and might not get along all the time, but Mr. Prince Charming knew Oscar would keep me safe.

"I'll tell him after I go see Bella," I said. She was the one who helped me understand what each charm meant.

Bella Van Lou owned Bella's Baubles, the only jewelry store in Whispering Falls. No doubt Mr. Prince Charming had gotten the charm from her. Every charm he'd ever given me had come from her.

The bell above the door dinged. Mr. Prince Charming ran over and rubbed up against Faith Mortimer's leg.

"My goodness! It's getting cold out there." Faith rushed in, frigid air chased in behind her. She slammed the door. "And the wind isn't talking to me."

She bent down and picked up my furry cat. His purr grew louder with each swipe of her hand down his back.

I gnawed on the corner of my lip, my eyes lowered and I rubbed my hand down the front pocket of my jeans. I looked out the window and over the shops. The afternoon sky looked grey. Dark clouds formed over the tips of the mountainous background. A nervous feeling curled inside my stomach. My intuition told me something was brewing. Something that was not welcome in Whispering Falls.

The cackle of customers and happy faces skewed my view as they walked by on the sidewalk in front of the shop.

"Looks like we are going to have some customers." Faith interrupted my thoughts and set Mr. Prince Charming back on the ground. "You can run on and do your errands." Faith was more than capable of holding down the fort while I hurried down to see Bella and make good on my promise to see Patience. "I'm ready to take over."

"I won't be long." I assured her and headed back to the coat tree to grab my cloak. I grabbed the edges and snapped it out in front of me before I wrapped it around me and tied the straps around my neck. I grabbed Madame Torres and my bag, stowing her deep at the bottom.

"Can I drop the holiday cheer?" I heard Madame Torres snap from the bottom of the bag.

Without looking in my bag, I gave the ball a quick smack with the pads of two fingers, shutting her up. The music turned off.

"If you need something, just holler. I'll be in the village." I didn't exactly want to tell her what I was up to. Faith might accidentally let it slip if I did tell her I had a new protection charm. It was a risk I didn't want to take. Oscar had enough on his plate and I was sure I could figure this out on my own.

I put the strap of my bag across my body while making my way through the customers looking at all the homeopathic bottles.

I opened the door and stepped out, grabbing the edges of the cloak and wrapping it tighter around me to ward off the nippy, chilling air. Only I realized the chill was still from deep within my soul.

CHAPTER FIVE

"Hmmm." Bella Van Lou was hunched over the glass counter at Bella's Baubles looking at the brass bell charm through the loupe. "He definitely picked a different charm this time."

Bella shivered from her toes to her hair follicles. So much so the bracelets around her wrists jingled.

"What was that?" I eyed her suspiciously.

"What?" She flipped her head to the side, letting her long blond hair fling over her shoulder.

"That shiver." I pointed my finger at her, outlining her body.

"Chilly." She crossed her arms, rubbing her hands up and down her arms. She gave a slight smile that didn't show the gap between her teeth nor was the smile the kind that balled her cheeks. This kind of smile I didn't need my intuition to tell me that she was hiding something.

"Chilly? Really?" I leaned forward and planted my hands on the glass counter and bent down a bit since Bella was five-foot-two, bringing myself nose-to-nose with my friend. "After all we have been through, you are going to tell me you are chilly?"

Bella took a step back. Her smoky eyes showed a slight, watchful hesitation. Her throat moved up and down. Her mouth parted, she put her tongue between the gap in her two front teeth like she did when she was nervous.

"You are doing that thing with your tongue." I pointed to her mouth.

"What thing?" She pinched her lips together.

"That tongue thing. Between your teeth." I twirled my finger in front of her mouth. "That thing you do when you're nervous." I planted my hands on my hips. "If you know something, just tell me."

"*Ahem*," she cleared her throat. "This is one charm I wish he hadn't picked out." She sniffed through her nose.

A creepy uneasiness found its way in the bottom of my heart. I sucked in a deep breath. I had to face it. I was a witch. How bad could it be?

"I'm ready." I straightened back up and pulled my shoulders back. My cloak fell behind my shoulders and hung on my back. The tie made me feel like I was choking but I wasn't about to adjust it. I needed to be strong.

"The bell is a symbol for letting you know something is coming or has come, like the bell over doors. It lets you know someone is there. But the brass is another story." She used her finger to push the small brass bell charm on the glass counter toward me. "Brass helps protect from falling for the evil eye, from evil spirits and any sort of spell cast against you."

"Spell cast against me?" I giggled at the thought, knowing that was virtually impossible since casting spells was against the by-laws.

"Have you made anyone mad lately?" Bella asked as if she were giving me a hazy warning. The look on her face told me she wasn't kidding.

"Mad?" My head jerked side-to-side. "Who on earth could be mad at me?"

"Well, your wedding was less than what was promised." She shrugged.

"My wedding?" I drew my hand up to my chest. "It was amazing."

Okay, maybe it wasn't what Oscar and I had planned. The town was crazy excited about the union between Oscar and I. It was a match the spiritual gods had to create since Oscar was a Dark-Sider Spiritualist and I was a Good-Sider Spiritualist. Dark-Siders were known to have a bit of an evil side, but there were good ones like Oscar and Eloise Sandlewood. Even Faith's sister was a Dark-Sider, long story short…her parents had a multi-spiritualist union like Oscar and me. And if Oscar and I had children, one of them could. . .

"Oh my God!" I gasped. "What if it's Aunt Helena?"

"Your own aunt would put a spell on you?" Bella asked in a *really, no way, what are you talking about, are you crazy* tone.

"It might seemed far-fetched, but look at what happened when I met Raven and Faith when I was a student at Hidden Halls, A Spiritualist University." My brows rose. "They come from a multi-spiritualist family and Aunt Helena had a problem with it."

"They were causing havoc at the university." Bella didn't see what I was saying. "Even though they were each trying to keep the other safe."

It was true. It had been set up to look like Raven had almost killed Faith when Faith was poisoned, but really it was a different evil force.

"Helena didn't do it." Bella reminded me how my own aunt wasn't a killer.

"I'm not saying she's a killer, maybe she put a little hex on me not to get pregnant." A deep sigh escaped me, lifting my shoulders up and then down.

"Pregnant?" Bella looked a little frazzled. "How did we go from multi-spiritualist relationships to pregnancy?"

"Think about it." I knew it was off, maybe way off. "Aunt Helena was so mad about me not having the ancestral dance performed at midnight and because Oscar isn't a Good-Sider, I wasn't about to do it." I ran my hands through my hair. "And we all know how the wedding plans had changed."

Even though Aunt Helena didn't say it or act like it, I could tell she wasn't happy when I went to my bridal shower, the night before the wedding, and through a strange turn of events Oscar and I got married that night at an impromptu ceremony. It ended up being perfect for us, but not the wedding my only living relative wanted me to have.

"You've got to be kidding?" Bella reached across the counter, grabbed my wrist and clipped my charm bracelet off of me. "There is no way."

"I'm just saying she doesn't want me to have children yet. Especially one that could be part Dark-Sider. Or full." The thought of Aunt Helena possibly doing something like this was ridiculous.

She would never put a spell or hex on me. But who would?

"You're right. She does love Oscar, just not his heritage and she did look like she was having a good time after we tied the knot." The fond memories of my wedding night still didn't override the feeling that something was not right. "But what about that?"

I gestured to the charm she was putting on my ever-growing protection bracelet.

"I don't know. But I do know that he," I followed Bella's finger past my shoulder and out her front window where Mr. Prince Charming was sitting on the outside windowsill. "He knows what is best and this." She dangled the bracelet in the air. "This is obviously what you need to keep you safe at this moment."

CHAPTER SIX

"Well, well." I looked at Mr. Prince Charming who was patiently waiting for me on the steps outside of Bella's Baubles. I shook my wrist back and forth letting the charms jingle against each other. "Happy?" Sarcasm dripped out of my mouth.

I'd have been much happier if he hadn't dropped the charm by my foot.

"I told you it's a bad idea," Gerald Regiula's voice echoed across the street from the front of The Gathering Grove Tea Shoppe. His back was to me, but Petunia Shrubwood faced him. "This is not our holiday."

"But I think it will be good for the tourists who do come for the bazaar," Petunia insisted in a loud voice.

Gerald shook his head and turned his body toward the street. Baby Orin was strapped to him in one of those front backpack looking things new moms use to keep their baby snugged tight to them.

"They come to the bazaar for our shops. To help our economy. Not some. . ." Gerald threw his arms in the air, "some carnival rides in the cold!" His lips flapped together in a fluster.

"It's just another added bonus for them to stay in town." Petunia stomped her foot. Her usually messy brown hair was much messier today. A few holly berries dropped out of her hair. A couple of birds came out of nowhere, swooping down and plucked them in their mouths.

I tried to hear more of their conversation, but I couldn't make it all out. All I knew was that Petunia wanted to bring a carnival to the bazaar and Gerald didn't. They were definitely arguing.

"Keep your voice down," Petunia whispered, her eyes gazed toward me and then she leaned into Gerald. "June is right there."

Gerald glanced across the street. My hand shot up in the air. There was no way I could ignore them. It was a small village and if I ignored them, they'd know I heard them.

"Hi!" I waved. I darted across the street, avoiding a couple of cars driving down Main Street. Mr. Prince Charming made it over to them before I did. "Look at sweet baby Orin. Isn't that adorable?"

I ran my finger over the top of the small baby black top hat that matched the one on Gerald perfectly.

"Thank you," Petunia had pulled Orin's baby blanket up clear to his eyes.

"Can I see his sweet face?" I asked and smiled.

"No." Petunia shook her head. Her hair was falling down from the usual top-knot. Half of her hair was up and half was down, not on purpose. It just looked like she had gotten out of bed and walked down the street. "Keeping the chill off of him."

"Yes." Gerald barked underneath his mustache. "Chill off of him."

Gerald and Petunia's glances interchanged again. Petunia continued to tuck the blanket even tighter around Orin. She acted like an anxious child who had stumbled upon something she shouldn't have. Or maybe I had stumbled upon something or a conversation they didn't want me to hear.

"Oh." I gestured my finger up and down Gerald's typical outfit of black suit with grey pinstripes and tux tails. "You should get Orin a little outfit like yours." I winked trying to break the ice, only a haunting suspicion told me they didn't want to hear my chitchat.

"Is everything okay?" I asked, noticing the dark circles under Petunia's eyes.

Baby Orin had really rocked their little spiritual world. They were used to caring for each other and Petunia was used to caring for the four-legged creatures of the community.

"It's fine." Petunia's chin nodded up and down fast. "All fine." She grabbed Gerald by the elbow and jerked it toward her. "We have a village council meeting this afternoon, we must go or we will be late."

"Oh, yeah!" I had forgotten all about the meeting. "Oscar will be there. Do you want me to babysit Orin?"

"That would be great!" Gerald puffed up.

Petunia jerked her hand from the crook of his elbow and smacked his arm. "No she cannot!"

"But June loves Orin. She might be able to help," he muttered under his breath and turned his head away from me as though I couldn't hear him.

"I can help." I rocked back and forth on my heels. My intuition was nagging me, but I buried the feelings deep in my toes. I could see there was something wrong. I didn't know what, but something was happening between them and if I could take baby Orin while they went to the meeting, then I would.

Petunia crossed her arms and jammed her hands under her armpits. Gerald unhooked the straps of the baby carrier and handed it to me with Orin tucked inside. Before I could protest, Gerald had that thing strapped across my body and snapped in the back. Baby Orin hung on me like a baby kangaroo Joey. I tugged on my bag underneath Orin and moved it around my body, letting it rest on my back.

"Ah." I peeled back the cover to get a look at the sweet sleeping baby and nearly fell over. "Oh." My voice fell flat.

"See!" Petunia reached toward the snuggly bundle. Gerald smacked her hands away. "She will tell the world."

"What happened?" I asked when I noticed Orin had a full man's mustache. Now I hadn't been a spiritualist long enough to see any of the villagers have children, but I did know that babies weren't supposed to have full mustaches. "I mean, he's cute, but what happened?" My lip curled and I leaned my head to the right to get a better look.

Mr. Prince Charming jumped on his hind legs and put his front paws on my thigh to get a better look.

"And him." Petunia buried her head in her hands.

"We don't know what happened." Gerald chest heaved up and down. "He woke up that way a couple of days ago. We went to the doctor in the middle of the night, but he knew nothing."

I didn't even know where parents went to see a pediatrician, especially a spiritualist pediatrician. It was going to be a long time before Oscar and I even talked about having a baby.

"But we love him." Petunia stepped up between me and Gerald. Her eyes filled with tears.

"I know you do." I put a flat palm on Orin's back and my other hand rubbed up and down Petunia. "You have people here who love you and want to help out."

"If the doctor can't help us, who can?" Petunia cried. "And look at me." She used both hands to push her hair back up in the messy updo I was used to seeing her in. She used one of the twigs like a Chinese chopstick to keep it up.

A bird popped its head out from underneath the massive head of hair and dove right back in. A feather floated down next to Petunia. Gerald grabbed it out of the air and held it toward me.

"Orin loves his face to be brushed with feathers." He pushed it in my face.

I took it from him and stuck it down in my bag.

"What did the doctor say?" I asked.

"I told you, he said he didn't know." Gerald's voice muffled and quieted as people walked by. Constance Karima was one of them.

Her eyes met mine. Hers lowered, mine popped open. Then she gave me a suspicious sideway glance as if telling me she wasn't happy I hadn't stopped by to see Patience. Really with Constance away at the village council meeting, it would be much better. I really did have a clue what was going on with Patience.

"Did Orin have tests run or . . ." I shook my head trying to grab for any sort of ideas that came to me. But I had nothing. I knew nothing about babies.

"Orin is not a mortal baby," Gerald's voice lifted. Petunia kept her hands on her face. "They just don't do tests like they do where you grew up."

"Oh." I decided to keep my questions to myself. They were on edge and they obviously didn't want my opinion, which really meant nothing since I had no experience raising any kind of baby. Still, I did plan on trying to help them any way I could.

"We have to go. Are you sure you don't mind watching him?" Gerald asked.

"I'm positive. I love this little guy." I looked down at Orin sleeping soundly. He was still just as cute with the man-mustache. Cuter.

Both parents gave me a concerned look.

"I'm fine." I put one hand on each of them and pushed them away from me and Orin. "Go! You are going to be late."

"I don't even want to go," Gerald scoffed and rolled his eyes.

"I bet June would like a little winter carnival." Petunia sounded confident on what I might like. "Right, June? I believe you were mortal once. They love a carnival."

"I did." I smiled trying to keep the peace. It was hard to dampen the memory of the sweet, delicious tastes of funnel cakes and gooey, fattening elephant ears.

"See! And most of our tourists are women. All are mortals." Petunia had a good point.

I nodded.

"What is exactly going on?" I had bits and pieces put together but not the whole picture.

"Petunia called an emergency council meeting to get a sudden change in the bazaar plans approved." Gerald looked at his wife and then back to me.

"I think it would bring more people to the bazaar as well as keep them here longer which turns into more money for the village econo-my." Petunia shrugged.

"That is what this emergency meeting is about?" I questioned, finding it odd they would need to meet on such a decision.

"Yes." Gerald's brows lifted. "I guess we better get going before we are late." Gerald rubbed baby Orin's back. "It wouldn't be good if the village president was late."

Gerald put an arm around Petunia. To anyone else it would look as though he was keeping her warm from the cold air, but I knew he was comforting her about two things. First was her worry about baby Orin staying with me and second was the fact she was worried about why he had grown a mustache.

I snugged Orin tight to my body and even covered him more with the edges of my cloak as I watched Gerald and Petunia cross the street and disappear between A Charming Cure and Magical Moments on their way to The Gathering Rock.

The Gathering Rock was behind A Charming Cure up the hill between the shop and my cottage. There was a big rock and a cleared area where all the village meetings and gatherings were performed. Normally I was asked to give a cleansing using my special sage sticks, but not this time. If it was just a vote about a silly carnival, there was no need to cleanse.

Maybe subconsciously I knew that's why they hadn't asked me, so my intuition wasn't going off, but my insecure meter was. Who knew? All I did know was that Mr. Prince Charming had given me a brass bell charm to ward off evil and baby Orin looked like an old man.

CHAPTER SEVEN

Two Sisters and a Funeral was located on the edge of town. It was a two-story Victorian red brick house, typical of mortal funeral homes. It was the only building that didn't look like the rest of Whispering Falls, nor did it have a fun gate with a walkway. It was a typical southern looking funeral home. The large Victorian home with big glass windows and a large covered gathering porch on the front. The inside of Two Sisters had the same look. Heavy and thick dark crown molding framed the walls along with thick threaded wall-to-wall carpet. The entrances of the rooms were large and also outlined in the heavy dark crown molding.

I had never been to a full funeral service at Two Sisters, but from what I had heard, Constance and Patience had a way of making the service feel more like a celebration of life instead of death. Everyone walked away from A Two Sisters and a Funeral services, saying they felt their loved one was there and it was a little...well...*magical*.

"Come on," I said in a hushed whisper to Mr. Prince Charming. There was no way I was going to go in there alone. There was just something about going in a place where dead bodies were hanging out. Not to mention ghosts.

Constance and Patience Karima's spiritual gift was helping the dead get to the other side. I was sure that was how families felt like they were celebrating their loved one's life instead of the end.

"I said to come on." Mr. Prince Charming was standing on the bottom step of the funeral home and not budging. I lifted my hand in the air and wiggled my wrist, the bracelet jingled. "You got me into this. Come on," I demanded through my gritted teeth. "I'm not going in there without my fairy-god cat." My brows lifted. "Got it?"

I opened the door and Mr. Prince Charming reluctantly ran in ahead of me.

I stepped into the long wide and dark hallway. The walls were draped in long deep-red fabric that hung from ceiling to floor. I couldn't imagine dusting those things. The pale yellow carpet with small red diamond designs lined the floors. Four large heavy ornamental wooden doors, two on each side, were shut. The massive staircase at the end opened up to a wraparound balcony.

"Get back here!" Patience screamed, but she was nowhere to be seen.

Thunderous footsteps boomed overhead. I looked up. Patience's pet ostrich jolted across the balcony above. His neck swooping forward with each step and loose feathers flew behind him.

"Stop!" Patience wobbled after him a few seconds later. She stopped in mid-wobble. One foot planted firmly on the carpet while the other was stuck in mid-air behind her. Her head slowly turned toward me and looked down. She clipped her mouth together and planted the other foot.

She pushed her glasses up on her nose. She squeezed her beady little eyes at me and huffed. The hot air came out of her nose and fogged up her glasses.

"What are you doing here? Constance isn't here." Her arms hung down her sides and she picked at the edges of her orange housedress. "And what the hell is that?" She pointed to baby Orin.

"And it's baby Orin." I twisted my body so she could see. Her face contorted. "With a hat." I said like it was normal to put a top hat on a baby. "And he has a mustache." I shrugged. "Guess what's coming to the village for the bazaar?"

I knew Patience would be the first of us spiritualists in line at the carnival. She loved to have fun in a child-like kind of way even though she was elderly.

Out of nowhere, a small yellow ball bounced down the stairs and landed right next to Mr. Prince Charming.

Rowl! Mr. Prince Charming jumped, twisted in the air, batted the ball and hid behind my legs.

"That!" I pointed to the ball. "That!"

"I. . .um. . .I," Patience hurried as much as she could hurry, pumping her arms as she bolted down the hallway.

I darted up the stairs with Mr. Prince Charming right behind me.

"Oh, no you don't!" I screamed darting down the hall after her. "If you want me to take you to the carnival, you have to answer some questions about that ghost boy!"

The door at the end of the hallway closed. Immediately I went to that door and opened it, even though the feathers had stopped at a different door.

When the door was fully opened, the shock of what was inside nearly knocked me over. A room full of caskets lined up, one after the other. Color after shiny color made me dizzy.

I put my hand on the doorknob and yanked the door back to me. I turned and planted my back against the door. What stood on the other side of that door gave me the full on heebie jeebies.

Mewl. Mr. Prince Charming taunted me from the hallway. I swear he had a smile on his face as if he was saying *I told you not to come in this funeral home.*

"Why?" I asked. "Why do I have to have fairy-god anythings that are so unhelpful?"

Madame Torres and Mr. Prince Charming loved giving me a hard time. I doubt anyone else had that problem. Oscar carried a wand in his gun holster and I never saw him even have to use it but once. It never gave him a bit of trouble that time. He pulled it out, pointed it and it worked. No fuss. No back talk. No nothing.

Mr. Prince Charming must've felt bad because he walked in and out between my ankles doing his signature figure-eight move that told me going into the casket room was going to be okay.

I closed my eyes, sucked in a deep breath through my nose and ignored the smell of death that shot into my lungs, and let out a long steady stream of air through my mouth. I closed my eyes, turned the doorknob and flung the door open.

"Patience, I'm not playing." I planted my feet firmly on the ground and put my hands on baby Orin. He was getting fidgety. I was sure my heart rate had woken him up from his deep sleep. Or at least caused him to stir. "I won't take you to the carnival. I can't wait to bite into a crispy, juicy caramel apple. They are so juicy I have to wipe my chin so many times from the dripping goodness."

All the caskets were sitting on top of the church carts, gurneys, but the one rattling caught my eye.

With my eyes trained on the chattering death box, I slowly made my way over to it and knocked on top the silvery steel casket.

"Go away!" Patience screamed from inside.

"Okay, so your sister came to me and said you were going nuts," I put my mouth closer to the closed casket. It was time to come clean. "I don't think you are nuts. I think you have more going on with your spiritual gift than you care to tell anyone."

I backed up when I saw the top begin to open.

"I think you've always had Constance to rely on and you've never had your own spiritual experience," I said.

It was true. Every personal experience I had ever had with the twins was always the result of something Constance had said or done. Patience just stood behind her agreeing with everything she had said.

The top fully opened and Patience lay in the cream, silk lined casket with her hands neatly crossed over her torso like she was the owner of the deathbed.

"You might be right," she squeaked out.

"I know I'm right," I said and pointed to my gut. "I know I'm not supposed to read other spiritualists, but you are blinking like one of them Las Vegas casino signs. Not only to me, but also to Constance. She knows something is going on and she wants me to fix you."

Patience sat up. She used her fingers to fluff out her tight-knit curls on the back of her head that had been flattened while hiding in the casket.

"I don't know what to do." She wrung her hands.

"You have to let me help you." I put my hands out to help her out of the casket.

"No." She smacked my hands away. "I can get out of here without your help. I'm talking about the you-know-what."

"I can help you with both." I grabbed her hands and helped her out of the casket. "I can certainly help you with your little ghost problem."

"He won't go away. No matter how much I ignore him." Her eyes darted to the door and the yellow ball bounced in. A little giggle escaped her and she kicked the ball back to the door.

"You encourage him." I looked back at the door and didn't see anything but the ball. I wasn't privy to seeing ghosts and that was fine with me. I think that would be almost as bad as being a funeral home director like the Karimas. "You can't laugh at him and expect him to leave you alone. Besides, aren't you supposed to help him go to the other side?"

"He won't go." She hung her head down and shuffled her toe on the carpet. "I don't even know where he came from."

Her answer had hammered me. "What?" I asked. "How can you tap into your gift and not help?"

"I don't know." She shook her head. "I've always done it with Constance, but she doesn't see him."

The him she was referring to was a little boy. He loved playing with the yellow ball and messing with the other spiritualists. In fact, he almost ruined my wedding.

It was not a secret that Aunt Helena and Eloise didn't see eye to eye on the type of wedding Oscar and I should have since both of them were the only living relatives we had. Both wanted to preserve our heritage and hadn't been willing to budge on the rituals. The little ghost boy loved to hang around Mr. Prince Charming, but my ornery cat clearly didn't like the little boy. I had no idea this little boy was around. I had mentioned out loud to Mr. Prince Charming how I wished I could have the wedding I wanted for my heritage, and the little ghost boy heard me, poisoning Eloise. Not enough to kill her but enough to make her sick on the eve of my wedding during my bridal shower. I ended up putting two and two together and figured out the yellow ball belong to a ghost. Not to mention I had caught Patience talking to the ball. Then I knew she saw him. Luckily I was able to give Eloise a potion to undo the poison.

The only good thing that did come out of that whole poisoning thing, Aunt Helena and Eloise saw that my union with Oscar was far more important than some little ritual.

"This is a problem," I said referring to Constance not seeing the little boy.

"He is awful." Her nose curled. "He plucked the ostrich's feathers. He taunts him and even tries to poke him in the eyes. He only does it when Constance is around."

"That is why she thinks you've gone crazy." The ball rolled back toward us and stopped at my feet. I ran my hands over baby Orin when he moved.

Orin lifted his little head, opened his eyes, and a big smile made his little man mustache curl.

"You shouldn't have brought Orin with you." Patience's eyes shot open. Her head slowly moved side to side. "He likes babies," her tone sent chills up my spine.

"Okay." I wanted to give her some sort of hope. "I will help you get him to the other side. I don't know how, but I will. All I'm asking you to do is not pay attention to him when Constance is here. If you need a place to hang out, come see me."

There was only one place I knew to look. The Magical Cures Book, the grimoire, Darla had left me.

CHAPTER EIGHT

Baby Orin was getting a little restless. I assured Patience I would get back to her once I found something to help her get the little ghost boy where he needed to go. I tucked the edges of my cloak around Orin's snuggie and held my hand close to his head. Trying to jingle my bracelet to keep him occupied and bounce while I walked down the street was a difficult task, only assuring me that children were far off for me and Oscar.

My efforts were proving to be fruitless.

"June! Wait!" Raven Mortimer was standing underneath the awning on the sidewalk in front of Wicked Good Bakery. Her long black hair was draped over her right shoulder. Her black embroidered Wicked Good Bakery apron was nearly white from all the flour splashed all over it. She held a silver pan in her hands.

"I can't stop!" I called halfway across the street toward A Charming Cure. "I've got Orin and he's fit to be tied."

"But I have something to tell you!" She had a bland ball of dough in her fist, not uncommon for her to have in her hands.

"I know! I know!" I lifted my hand in the air and wiggled my bracelet back and forth.

"But I need to talk to you now!" she insisted. The dough squeezed through her fingers.

I stopped at the urgency of her voice and looked back at her. Orin let out another scream, sending my feet in a forward motion.

"Not now!" I waved her off and headed to the gate. "It's going to be okay," I said in my best baby voice and put my hand on the gate to A Charming Cure.

The most god-awful, blood-curling scream came out from under the man-mustache; it made me detour around the shop and up the hill. Orin was not happy when he noticed I was not his mother or father.

"It's okay. We are going to see your mama," I assured the little guy.

Petunia was addressing Izzy, Gerald, Oscar, and Chandra and a few other people I didn't recognize. Orin had calmed down the squeal to a gurgle so I decided to stand in the back. Petunia and I made eye contact. I smiled to let her know everything was okay, even though it wasn't and I couldn't wait to get him unstrapped from me.

"I'm not sure this is a good idea." A man stood up from the crowd of people with his back to me. "It's not the rides kind of carnival. We will walk through the streets with some juggling, balloon tricks, sword swallowing. You know," the man's shoulders shrugged. "Light magic."

Light magic? Oh, the sound of that made my ears perk. We had never had other spiritualists join in on our bazaar. No wonder they needed to vote. But. . .

I gulped. Why hadn't they asked me to cleanse? I took a deep breath when my intuition started to go off. The smell of money curled around my body, down my nose and made me squeak. No matter how hard I tried, I couldn't take my eyes off the man.

The man stood about five-foot-eight, thinly built and had on a blue overcoat. It was a coat I had just seen this morning. The man's words stopped when he turned around to address the crowd and our eyes met.

"You," I gasped when I pinned him as the customer I had made a potion for earlier this morning at A Charming Cure.

His face clouded with uneasiness. A warning voice whispered in my head, causing me to become dizzy. When I became dizzy, I knew what followed. Passing out. I sucked in a few quick breaths.

"Not now," I repeated and made circles on baby Orin's back with the palm of my hand. "Not with baby Orin strapped to you," I talked myself out of my dizzy spell. Or it could've been the crazy mixture of a rapid heart rate and the bitter cold taking over my body.

Like a lightning rod, the man bolted from The Gathering Rock circle and disappeared into the wooded area.

"Wait!" I screamed and snugged baby Orin close to me. I ran after him, as best I could without jiggling the baby around too much. "You! You wait!" I screamed, waving my arm in the air.

He was obviously a spiritualist from somewhere, and he knew that when he came into my shop. If anyone found out I had made him a special potion, I'd be in a lot of trouble.

The trees on the edge of the woods parted on my arrival. I stopped, turned around and noticed Petunia, Gerald and Oscar were running after me.

As if frozen in time, the Whispering Falls Gazette came through with the bitter breeze.

Hear ye, hear ye. The winds have spoken, the chill hangs in the air. Hopefully the winter bazaar will be a great success for the village once again! We welcome the spiritual carnival. This update is brought to you by Glorybee Pet Shop and Village President Petunia Shrubwood who brought this wonderful carnival to town. Faith's voice faded off when the snap of branches cracked in the distance.

"Him." My eyes darted between the depths of the woods and the thunderous footsteps behind me.

"June! Wait!" Oscar yelled from behind me. There was a tense shrill to his voice.

I did the exact opposite. I ran toward the sounds of the breaking branches deep within the woods.

The towering trees began to shed what leaves they had left and they rained down on me. The owl hooted. The sky turned grey. Suddenly I felt suffocated as if the branches were curling around me.

I stopped. The air was thin. My chest heaved up and down. It felt as if I was struggling against something. Struggling to breath. Struggling to move. Struggling. . .

"June! What have you done?" Oscar scrambled over to me. His eyes drew down to my feet, causing me to look.

"I. . .I. . ." The words were struggling to come out of my mouth. The man was lying on the ground next to my feet. My potion bottle in his grip.

"Fresh body," Constance Karima's voice escalated. She lifted her nose in the air and took a few quick inhales through her nose. Eagerly she rubbed her hands together. Excitement exuded from her. Her aura even glowed. "I must get Patience and the ambulance."

I glared at her as she scurried off in the direction of Whispering Falls.

"Give me him." My body jerked as Petunia grabbed the snuggly pack from my body.

Oscar's eyes met mine. My body stiffened with shock.

"June Heal." Three little bodies floated down from the tops of the trees and hovered over the man's body. All three of them cross-legged, arms folded, and six eyes staring at me.

I gulped. Hearing the Order of Elders say my name made my stomach hurt. They only showed up when something was wrong. Clearly, something had gone very wrong.

"Yes," my voice died away. I looked between all three Marys. Mary Ellen, Mary Lynn, and Mary Sue made up the trio.

At the same time their legs uncurled. Gracefully they floated to the ground, landing on their black pointy-heeled boots.

"He's dead." The chill hung on Mary Ellen's words. "You are hereby confined to Whispering Falls, pending the investigation of the death of this man," her voice cracked.

She cocked her leg to the side and slowly drew her arms down her skintight black unitard and past her toes. She planted her finger on the guy's neck before jerking back up to standing.

Her dark lashes cast a shadow on her face as she drew them open and focused on me. Her eyes slightly closed, her lips pursed. The lingering eyes of Chandra, Izzy, Gerald, Constance, and Oscar stared at the man while Petunia cradled baby Orin, singing in his ear.

CHAPTER NINE

"I didn't do it." I paced back and forth in front of Oscar's desk in the police station.

"June, please sit." Oscar pointed to the chair.

"I can't sit." If Oscar or anyone else there staring at me thought I was going to just sit there and let it look like I had killed that man, they were nuts. "I didn't do it."

"It sure looks like you did," Chandra's eyes narrowed. "I mean, your bottle was in his hand. A bottle that you put your special gift in."

Everyone knew that my intuition potion bottles were different than the bottles the basic homeopathic cures are in.

"And how did he get your bottle without coming into your shop? The special potion bottle?" Izzy tapped her chin with her long skinny finger. She swooped around, her A-line polka dot orange and black dress twirled, and came face-to-face with me. Her long blond hair swept behind her shoulders. "June," she gasped, "you didn't make him a special potion?"

I gulped.

"Answer the question, June," The Marys said in unison. Mary Sue's voice more brash than the others.

"He came into the shop and he was looking around at my stress potions. When I walked closer, I smelled money."

"Money?" Petunia asked. Everyone looked at her and she clamped her mouth shut. When the Order of Elders speak, you are supposed to remain silent.

"Yes. Money," I confirmed. "I didn't mean to read him. My intuition took over and it did. If I'd known he was some sort of spiritualist in town, then I wouldn't have read him."

"Not only does this look like you murdered him by the evidence, but you also broke the first by-law." Mary Lynn stood four feet tall. She rubbed the fox stole around her shoulders with long, deliberate strokes.

"How was I supposed to know?"

"Did you read your intuition?" Mary Ellen strutted around the police station in her unitard. She coiled a strand of her long black hair around her finger. "Did you get chills, a pit in your stomach?" She pointed to her gut.

Chills? Pit? Did I. I had been having chills since I woke up. I grabbed my wrist and ran my finger over the brass bell charm.

"What?" Oscar asked, concern in his voice. He was good at reading me. His eyes drew down to my hand. "Did you get another charm?"

My eyes grew as my chin slowly lifted up and down.

"I woke up chilled to the bone. Goosebumps covered me from head-to-toe. It was as if I couldn't get my body temperature to come up."

The Marys stared at me, making me feel like I needed to keep talking. Which I did.

"I got this charm from Mr. Prince Charming." I held out my wrist. The Marys brought their heads together and at the same time dropped them down to take a look.

"Brass," each one of them gasped at the same time.

"And a bell," Mary Lynn squealed in a small voice. She dragged the palm of her hand in a long deliberate motion down her fur.

"Mmhmmm." Mary Sue's nose curled. She lifted her arm and uncurled her long finger toward me. "If you would've listened to your intuition of chills and body temperature. . ."

The sound of the ambulance caused us all to look out the police station window. The swirl and twirl of the siren screamed throughout the village. The Karima sisters had their heads stuck out the window of the ambulance on each side.

"You're fine. You aren't going to hit anything! Punch it!" Patience hollered out the window when the ambulance nearly sideswiped A Charming Cure trying to get up the hill to retrieve the body of the man. "We have a fresh body to get!"

"June, why didn't you tell me?" Oscar pulled me to the side while everyone was watching the Karima sisters try to get the ambulance up the hill. At one point Patience jumped out and used her arms to flag the way for Constance, who was driving. The whipping wind billowed out her housedress, making her look like one of those orange windsock flags you see at the airports.

"I didn't want to bug you because I didn't even know what it meant. I just found out today that there was some sort of evil lurking. And it was after he came to the shop," I said as fast as I could in a low whisper. "He didn't want me to know he was a spiritualist."

"At least I would've known and been on alert." Oscar made sense and it was something I had never thought of. "We are married now. You cannot go around keeping your intuition to yourself. And you won't go around trying to figure out who did this."

"But. . ." I protested. He knew me all too well.

"There is no but and I mean you keep your head out of all of this until I can get all of it figured out myself. The right way." He tapped his sheriff's badge.

"Or not." Colton Lance appeared behind Oscar. He stood around six-foot-three with big brown eyes and messy blond hair. There was a pretty young woman with long red hair standing next to him. She was not Ophelia Biblio, Colton's better half.

Colton and Ophelia had moved to Whispering Falls from a village out west when Oscar had lost his memory for what seemed like forever. Oscar had given up his heritage and all his powers to save me, yet again. Luckily, I was able to get a potion that helped him remember and since he wasn't technically a spiritualist when I did it, I didn't break any rules. Still, Colton and Ophelia fit into the village perfectly and the village council made Colton and Oscar both sheriffs, splitting the job.

On Oscar's days off as sheriff in Whispering Falls, he was a deputy in our former town of Locust Grove. If he had to work a long shift, he would stay in his old house but that was rare.

"This is Cecil Buviea." Colton introduced the woman. "She is the attorney for the carnival and will be handling the case of Paul Levy."

"Paul Levy?" I asked. Oscar put his hand in front of me. His eyes gave me the death stare, telling me to zip my lips.

"Who is Paul Levy?" Oscar asked.

"He's the man she killed." The woman drew her arm in the air and pointed her long green fingernail directly at me. "And there is no way we feel you," her eyes drew up and down Oscar, "will be able to help put her behind bars due to the nature of your relationship. That is why we have asked Sheriff Lance to take over the investigation. And we want her in jail!"

"Jail?" My jaw dropped.

"June Heal is a pillar in our village," Izzy took a step forward in my defense. She pushed back her long hair and ran her bony fingers down her A-line skirt.

"Our rules are as follows." Mary Ellen snapped her fingers and a scroll appeared in the air. She reached up and retrieved it pulling the scroll apart, she read, "According to the Spiritual By-Laws," she cleared her throat, pulled the scroll taut and held it close to her face. "When a spiritualist is accused of a crime, they are to be put on village arrest and unable to work in their shop or perform their spiritual gifts."

"That is not in our rules." The woman snapped back.

"Ms. Buviea, it is our rules." Mary Ellen's dark lashes flew down. "And you are in our world."

Our world? Mary Ellen's words felt like a punch to my gut. What did that mean?

"When we are guests in a town, we expect to be treated as such. Not come to town and have one of our own killed." Ms. Buviea stepped up and stood her ground with Mary Ellen, something I would have never done. "And we expect this, this," she turned her head and looked down her nose at me as if I were a piece of trash, "this so called pillar of the village to be taken into custody and jailed until the autopsy comes back."

As if on cue, the ambulance barreled down the hill and took a leap forward, twisting around in mid-air, landing on Main Street before zipping up the road, siren blaring as the ambulance made its way to Two Sisters and a Funeral. But not before I caught the glaring eye of one Constance Karima.

"God help me," I whispered, hoping I could at least get Patience's little problem cleared up so Constance would do everything in her power to find out the real cause of death.

Everyone stared at me. The chill from the outside had definitely made its way inside.

"Don't you dare jail my client!" Mac McGurtle stepped through the door. He wore a grey pinstriped suit. Thick black-rimmed glasses sat on his large nose. Underneath them his blue eyes zeroed in on Celia.

"Well, well, well." Celia lowered her voice in a mysterious way, "It looks like we finally get to have that match in court."

"Now, now." Colton Lance stood between them. "Hopefully it won't get to that."

"That's right." Celia stepped up. She leaned her body to the right, planted her hand on her hip, a long lean leg popped out from the split in the pencil thin skirt. "I have enough evidence to charge June Heal for the murder of Paul Levy. He came into her shop as he was strolling around the town, getting ready for his debut for your bazaar and she gave him a potion to kill him."

"I did no such thing." I protested, pulling my shoulders back.

"Did he or did he not come into your shop?" Her eyes snapped toward me. Her tone held venom.

"You can answer that question," Mac nodded.

"He did. But he didn't tell me he was a spiritualist." There had to be a way around this charade.

"You are a spiritualist that has the gift of intuition. You should have known by your gift. Unless you didn't fulfill your schooling." She turned her head toward Mac and lifted her brows.

"You can answer that." Mac nodded again.

"I finished a year and became village president." It was true. I had only gone to Hidden Halls, A Spiritualist University for one year and completed just enough to get by. But like she said, I used my intuition to work my magic.

"That is what most spiritualists do, Celia." Mac had decided to finally take up for me.

"Most spiritualists?" The edges of her lips turned up. "And you are saying June Heal is like most spiritualists?"

"We are all spiritualists." Mac shrugged. He used his thick finger and pushed his classes up on his nose.

The friendly banter between them apparently amused her. She threw her head back and laughed in a scornful tone.

"The June Heal. The Chosen One?" she asked, lowering her eyes.

"I. . ." I opened my mouth and nothing came out.

It was true but I had no idea what it truly meant. A while ago I had been named as the Chosen One between the Good-Siders and Dark-Siders. Something about me being able to move the spiritual world forward. I thought merging both worlds together and combining our laws, I had done what I was chosen to do.

CHAPTER TEN

I t took a lot of fast-talking for Oscar to even get through to Colton about setting me free under the law. The Marys refused to let Celia have me jailed and I was grateful for that, but not without them scolding me first.

You know better. You didn't listen to your intuition. You need to go back to University to a new intuition class.

Collectively, we all walked across the street to A Charming Cure where Colton and Oscar wanted to make sure there was no stone unturned.

"That is a splendid idea." Mary Lynn was the sweetest of the three. She looked like the little granny with her silver curls tousled around her head. She always wore a black suit and her fox stole. Her voice even dripped with sugar. She eased around A Charming Cure picking up bottles, opening them, testing the cures on her skin, before smelling them and sticking them back on the shelf. "We really all should take those continuing education classes like all the mortals do with their skills."

"Oh please," Mary Sue rolled her eyes before dipping her finger into my cauldron and giving it a good swipe. She lifted her fingertip to her nose and took a nice long whiff before she stuck the tip in her mouth. She smacked her lips together. "Tasty."

Oscar and Colton were busy scouring the shop for any clues Paul Levy had left behind and decided to do multiple tests on the cauldron, the Bushmaster snake, Thuja occidentalis, and the Calendula officinalis to see if there were some poison or other things besides what was supposed to be in there.

"June has wonderful intuition." Mary Sue couldn't help herself. She took another swipe of the inside of the cauldron tasting the potion. "And I'm telling you she didn't kill this guy." She drew her finger up and pointed toward Oscar and Colton who were waving their wands over the stress-free potion side of the shop for clues. "They are looking in the wrong place."

"You know as well as I do there are formalities among the worlds. This is a formality." Mary Ellen continued to pick up bottles and put them back, only she never put them back in the right place, which meant more work for me after they all left.

"I still think you need to go to more school." Mary Sue wasn't as forgiving as the others. She'd always been the brashest of the three and never let me off the hook for anything.

I wanted to protest everything they were saying, but I knew better. Any amount of bantering coming from me would only hinder their process more.

"I just can't ignore the facts." Colton held out his notebook and read from it. "Victim did come to your shop and didn't reveal self. Suspect used spiritual gift to read victim, breaking the village law. Suspect did not listen to own spiritual gift to realize victim was indeed a fellow spiritualist from another village, thus breaking the universal law." He paused to catch his breath and continued, "Victim was clearly upset when he saw suspect come to The Gathering Rock village meeting. Victim ran into the woods. Victim was found dead in the woods with the suspect standing over victim. Victim had suspect's potion in his grip and the potion smeared on his lips."

The entire shop fell completely silent.

"When you put it that way," I blurted out.

"It's just the facts, which is why I have to put you under village arrest." As soon as those words left Colton's mouth, the shop door flew open and Petunia Shrubwood rushed in with a scroll rolled up under her arm.

She handed Colton the scroll and left, never once looking me in the face.

"Well," Colton walked over. "I hate to do it, June, but I just can't let you leave until this gets figured out."

"I understand the rules." I tried to give him an understanding smile. "And I have no other place to go."

I stood silent as Colton read the ruling from the village president, only I wasn't listening. I was too busy remembering the fight between Gerald and Petunia outside of The Gathering Grove earlier this morning.

According to Gerald, Petunia was going to bat for the carnival to come to town. Why? What was her connection to Paul Levy?

Petunia Shrubwood, our very own president, knew something. And it was up to me to figure out what it was.

"What about the shop? You know you can't run the shop while the investigation is going on." Colton's words stung me to the core. The shop was all I had and it would be the only thing to occupy my time.

"I'm sure I can get Faith to come and help out." I couldn't believe this was happening. I loved this time of the year and here I was feeling the hatred in my soul.

"And stay here while you go to school?" Oscar's voice broke away.

"School?" My jaw dropped. Who was he to ask about school when he never finished his wizard classes?

Colton stepped up to talk but Oscar put his hand out for Colton to stop.

"I want to be involved so I have to tell her." There was tension between the two of them.

"Fine." Colton took a step back.

"June, you have to go back to school and take a class to continue the education. Levy's lawyer is requesting it and if we keep her at bay and happy, it gives us time to figure all this out." He waved his hand over the shop.

I stood there like a good wife and let Oscar tell me how it was going to go down. Only I didn't see it that way. It was going to go down exactly how my intuition told me it was. This was not the solution. I didn't know the solution, but I knew this was not it. And I knew I had to see Petunia.

"And what if I could get the village council to grant you a mini-honeymoon? Together." Colton had a painful look in his face like he hated to keep me in Whispering Falls under village arrest.

"There is no way I could leave." I looked over at the Marys who were gathered in a little circle testing out Black As Night lotion.

"Just think about it." Colton turned and went back to what he does best, policing.

My eyes narrowed. First Colton tells me I am under village arrest and then he turns around and offers Oscar and me a mini-honeymoon? A honeymoon was the last thing I needed. I needed to understand what was happening around me, starting with figuring out why Paul Levy was in my shop and how Petunia knew him. Where had he come from? Why me? Why did Paul and Petunia want the carnival here?

The thought rolled around in my gut. I let out a little laugh when my intuition told me if I could answer those questions, I would be on the path to freedom. But where?

CHAPTER ELEVEN

The fog circled around me. In the distance the familiar sound of Eloise's incense chain clinked in a rhythmic tempo. *Clink, clink, clink.*

The fog was so thick, I lifted my hands and parted it. The path ahead of me was clear, the glow of the carriage lights guided the way.

"June!" Raven called out. I jerked to the right. The fog danced around her as she gripped the ball of dough. The fog coiled around her neck and in a single tug, Raven fell to the ground.

"No!" I screamed reaching out into the fog, only it was a barrier. A barrier I couldn't reach through. "Raven!"

"It's not a good idea." Gerald's voice came from the left. I jumped around. He and Petunia were in the fog.

"I have to!" Petunia screamed. Her jaw locked.

"Do not let him in our life." Gerald warned and tried to grab Orin out of Petunia's arms.

Chooo, choooo. The lights of the train pierced the fog in front of Petunia and Gerald. The roaring train headed straight toward them. *Chooo, choooo.* The train's horn roared louder and louder, getting closer and closer to Gerald.

"Move, move, move," I whispered knowing they couldn't hear me. I closed my eyes right before the train barreled through the family of three. "No," I groaned.

Clink, clink, clink. The sound of Eloise's incense sang in the distance. The path in front of me was clear. The fog hung like a shield on each side of me.

"One, two, three, you are just like me," the sweet voice called me. It was like candy to my ear and hard to ignore. I took a couple of steps toward the laughter of children. The fog parted to the right and a juggler entertained a group of children standing on the sidewalk in front of Magical Moments. The juggler wore a green body suit with a face painted half white and the other half was painted the same green as the body suit. The juggler had on a joker hat that was white with green jingle bells hanging off the pointy edges. The juggler's shoes were identical to the hat with one big jingle bell on the pointy tip of the toe.

The children oohed and awed as the juggling pins climbed higher and higher into the sky. Out of nowhere the sound of the train echoed in the distance.

Chooo, chooooo. The roar got louder and louder.

"Oh no," I groaned, looking into the distance behind the children. "Move out of the way!" I screamed. "Move out of the. . ." I gulped and turned my head when the train came barreling down Main Street.

The screams of children and adults took up the deafening space in my head.

"I told you June is a Good-Sider!" Aunt Helena caused me to look up.

"She is marrying a Park! He's a Dark-Sider!" Eloise screamed back at her. Her hand lifted into the air. A big hot air balloon painted with the Blood Mercury flower. The hot air balloon popped. An explosion of water rushed down the main street like a tidal wave, sweeping the children up. The train disappeared.

"One, two, three, you are one of me." The voice swirled around Oscar. The tidal wave was going to swallow him up.

"No!" I thrashed back and forth trying to get the fog to break. "No!"

Something grabbed me from behind and twirled me around. It was Oscar, only his skin was sliding down, exposing a skeletal face.

"June! Wake up!" The voice called me. Oscar's voice. "June! It's just a dream!"

"It's just a dream," I whispered to the skeleton that had a grip on me. "You are not real," I cried. My eyes burned with hot tears. "Go away!" I jerked away from the skeletal fingers and opened my eyes.

"June," Oscar brushed my bangs back from my forehead. His eyes were searching mine. "There you are. Come back to me."

I blinked. My mouth was dry. My body convulsed.

"June, baby." Oscar pulled me up out of the bed and held my limp, exhausted body to him. He slowly rocked me back and forth. "It's okay," he whispered, sending me back to sleep.

CHAPTER TWELVE

"A re you okay?" Oscar asked, shuffling down the hall and rubbing his eyes.

"I'm fine," I lied in a much too chipper voice that sent an alarm to Oscar. The fact of the matter was, I was not okay.

Being the number one murder suspect in any murder case was not high on my list of okay situations. Plus the nightmare only solidified my fears that some evil was lurking in the foothills of our village.

Oscar kissed me gently on my forehead before reaching for his mug sitting on the counter next to the coffee pot.

"You're mad." Oscar leaned against the kitchen counter with his steaming coffee in one hand. He had to work in Locust Grove for the next twenty-four hours, giving me a little time to figure out my next move without him becoming suspicious. "I can tell by your attitude and tone of voice."

"I'm not mad." I insisted. Ok, another lie—I was roaring mad with my situation. After the nightmare I had had, I knew that I needed to figure out who killed Paul Levy and what grave danger Whispering Falls was facing.

"You came home last night and went to bed, only giving me a sweet kiss on the lips." He glanced over at Mr. Prince Charming. "Then the nightmare. When you are mad, you keep things from me."

Mr. Prince Charming was waving his tail in the air and dancing around my feet. Happy as could be.

But Oscar was right. He knew me all too well.

"If you were under house arrest for a murder you didn't commit, or had to go back to the university, you wouldn't be happy either." I grabbed a mug from the cabinet and filled my cup up. It was much easier to blame my bad attitude on being forced to go back to Hidden Halls instead of recalling all the images and feelings from my nightmare.

Meow. Mr. Prince Charming was in awfully good spirits for a fairy–god cat that needed to get me out of trouble.

"You and I both know that when you have a nightmare, it means only one thing." He set his mug down and propped himself up on the counter with his hand. "Your nightmares have a way of connecting the past events with future events."

"It's strange." I had to give him something. "I don't remember everything." The truth was, I was trying to forget most of the nightmare. It was one of the scariest I had ever had. Thinking about all my friends dying at the hand of something evil made me nauseous. "I just remember bits and pieces of me walking through town and hearing the chains on Eloise's incense."

"Really?" Oscar questioned.

I could tell he wasn't buying all of it.

"Yes, really." I threw it back at him. It was hard for me not to be a little upset that I wasn't able to go to my shop and do what I loved. Instead I had to go to school.

"I'm going to be late." I grabbed my bag and threw it over my body. "We are going to have to discuss this later. I can't be late for class because God knows what the Marys would do to me then." I reached for the door with Mr. Prince Charming by my side.

"Let me fix you a coffee," Oscar tried to stop me.

"I can get a coffee at Black Magic Café," I said referring to the coffee shop at Hidden Halls, A Spiritualist University. I ran out the door before he could stop me.

It wasn't that I didn't want to tell Oscar everything; I just wanted to make sure I was right before I sent him off into the world to fight my battles based on what could be accusations with no merit. My nightmares had had some accuracy before, but not exactly on target. I had to figure this out for myself.

"June! Come on!" He ran after me when I walked out the door. I tried to slam it behind me, but he caught it. "I'm on your side!" he yelled after me as I darted around the cottage and into the woods.

Mr. Prince Charming ran ahead of me to the wheat field.

"Trouble in paradise with what's his name?" Madame Torres asked from the bottom of my bag.

I dug my hand around the bottom and continued to walk to the wheat field, my portal out of Whispering Falls, and grabbed Madame Torres. She was covered in crumbs from being at the bottom of my bag.

"Gross." Madame Torres appeared in the glass globe. Her purple eye shadow was thick from her eyelashes to her eyebrows. The purple turban perched on top of her head had a lime green yellow gem in the center. She looked like she needed to be part of the traveling carnival here for the bazaar with her colorful display. "Do you need to keep me in the bottom of your bag?"

"His name is Oscar." I ran my hand over her globe to get off all the crumbs and particles of God knew what else that had collected in the bottom of my bag. "And if you were a little nicer, maybe I wouldn't just throw you in the bottom."

"Fine." Her voice dripped like a slow water drip, her eyes rolled back into her head. "How on earth are we going to get you out of this mess?"

"Aren't you my crystal ball? Look into the future? Tell me what to do?" I asked and shook my head.

Behind me the village was still at yawning peace. Ahead of me the tall wheat waved in the light morning wind. The chill in the air nipped at my neck. I pulled the edges of my cloak up around my neck and over the edges of my hair. Maybe it was good I wasn't able to make my appointment with Chandra. Unfortunately it was for awful reasons, but the longer hair was keeping some of the wind off my neck.

Mr. Prince Charming trotted ahead of me. I could only see the tips of his ears and the tip of his tail as it swayed along with the wheat as if he were dancing in the morning dawn. There was a distant line where the dark stopped and the light had begun. Soon all of Whispering Falls would be up and milling about in the warm sunshine of the chilly day. And without me.

"My plan is to play nice in the daylight and figure out who really killed Paul Levy," I said to Madame Torres just before the wooden sign popped out of the ground and several wooden arms shot out in all sorts of directions.

The wooded arrows pointed in different directions. Hidden Halls, A Spiritualist University had several different signs. Classes didn't start for a while and I wanted to get out of my cottage. Aunt Helena was probably up having her tea, so I touched the arm that showed me the way to the university.

Like magic, the wheat field parted and made the perfect path. At the end of the path, in the distance, the main street that ran through the university was just waking up with a few students walking around.

The first stop I had to make was Black Magic Café. There were only a couple of students ahead of me. The fresh smell of scones and coffee drifted through the café.

"What can I get ya?" Gus asked and wiped down the counter.

"I'll have a fresh blueberry scone and large coffee." I smiled when he looked up with a shocked look on his face.

He ran his hands through his ash blond hair. It was a lot less shaggy than normal. Gus Chatham had on his regular cargo shorts and surfer style look. He stood about six foot tall and was thin. His brown eyes sparkled when he smiled.

"I had no idea." He tapped his temple. Gus's spiritual talent was Clairvoyant Medium. He generally had a good idea when I was coming to visit at the university.

"I guess I threw you off." I winked. "I guess you haven't heard about my little trouble."

"No," he gasped and poured the large cup of coffee. "And by the sound of it, you need this." He pushed the cup toward me before he took the tongs and grabbed a fresh baked blueberry scone.

"Yum." My stomach growled. The blueberries were plump and a little soft and had the just out of the oven look. The top was lightly toasted brown and the edges had a nice crispness to them. "Looks delicious."

"They are." He slowly nodded his head. "I'll be right over."

I took a seat at one of the picnic tables. I had a choice of them all since the students coming and going were doing just that, going to class. Gus had walked over to another Black Magic Café employee and said something in her ear. He untied the apron from around his neck and took it off, putting it behind the counter.

"Trouble in paradise?" he asked as though Madame Torres had gotten to him.

"What makes you think that?" I asked, giving him the stink eye. I pinched off the edge of the scone and popped it in my mouth.

"Good, huh?" Gus smiled. "Anyway, you are here way too early for a newlywed." His brow cocked in a curious way.

"I have to come back to school." It was like eye rolling and the word school went together. Every time I said school, my eyes automatically rolled.

"Why?" His head pulled back.

"The Marys told me to." I pinched off a bigger piece this time and put it in my mouth. "There is a traveling carnival in Whispering Falls for the bazaar. One of them came into my shop. My intuition went off and I did what we do. I took care of him and sent him on his way."

"And?" Gus encouraged me to go on.

"I went on with my day. I did tell Constance Karima I would go see her sister. which I did, but not without telling Petunia I would babysit Orin." I smiled. Every time I said his name, his little man mustache popped into my memory.

"At least you are smiling." Gus returned the turned up mouth.

"Oh no." I shook my head and curled my hands around the hot cup of coffee. "I took Orin with me to see Patience Karima." I didn't bother telling him why I had gone to see Patience. It had nothing to do with why I was at the university. "Orin got a little restless, so I hurried to The Gathering Rock where there was an impromptu meeting Petunia was holding since she is the village president."

"I'm getting older every second you talk." Gus's head dipped, he stared at me with a pained expression. "Can you get to the reason you are here?"

"I am," I whined. "Anyway, the guy from my shop, Paul Levy." His name was forever engrained on my brain. "He was at the meeting. He saw me and took off. I followed him into the woods."

"You mean you ran after him to see why he didn't tell you he was a spiritualist too." He sucked in a deep breath and leaned back on the picnic table bench.

"Wait," I put my hand out in front of me and laid it on the table. "He was dead when I got there."

"Dead?" Gus's face contorted. Nervously he ran his hand through his hair. "Heart attack?" he asked with a quiver in his voice.

"No." I shook my head. "Well, maybe." I hadn't thought about that. "He had my potion bottle in his grip and there was evidence of it on his lips."

"Making you look like an immediate suspect?" His jaw jutted out, his eyes narrowed. "Unbelievable." He puffed through his nose. "And they just suspected you as the murderer?"

"The fact that he was fine and dandy moments before I found him looked bad. The potion was open in his hands and on his lips. Not to mention I completely broke rule number one of the by-laws." It just didn't look good. Hearing myself say it out loud made it sound even worse.

"When you lay it out like that, you're right. It doesn't look good." His eyes glanced over my shoulder. His chin jumped in the air. "I've got to go help out. It's getting busy."

He stood up and took a step toward the front of the café.

He stopped.

"But that doesn't tell me why you are here." His hand was planted on the picnic table.

"The lawyer for the traveling carnival insisted that I go to school to hone my craft while I'm on village arrest because I obviously broke the rules." I wanted to protest to him, but the fact was that I had broken the rules. Regardless my intuition told me to so maybe Celia Buviea was right. Maybe my intuition wasn't exactly right on target and I've just been lucky these past couple of years.

"June?" The familiar voice of Aunt Helena circled my head and into my ears.

I turned to see where she was. She stood on the sidewalk in front of Black Magic Café. She wore a long red cloak to match her pointy red boots. She waved. Her long red fingernails flashed up and down before she scurried over.

"To what do I owe this pleasure?" she asked.

I got up and hugged her. Tight. It felt like I was safe, comfortable, home.

"What is wrong?" she asked, squeezing me tighter to her. "I can feel the sorrow."

Without warning, tears sat on my eyelids and trickled down my face. She pushed me gently away and held me out at arms length. Fear rested in her eyes. She reached up and brushed the tears away from my cheek.

We sat down and I used the opportunity to ask the questions that had been swirling in my head.

"Aunt Helena, I have to ask you a very important question and I need a serious answer." I knew it was a long shot about her being behind any of my misfortunes lately, but the little tickle about the conversation I had with Bella in Bella's Baubles needed to be scratched.

"What is it dear?" she asked, rubbing her hand down my arm.

"I know that you were having an issue with my wedding to Oscar because of everyone wanting everyone to perform certain rituals." I didn't spell it out because she and I both knew what I was talking about. "Mr. Prince Charming brought me this charm and I can't help but think that with all the drama from the wedding, this could have something to do with it."

She stiffened. She drew her shoulders back. Her eyes pierced the distance between us.

"I mean the whole Good-Sider and Dark-Sider having a baby and not knowing what spiritual gift they might possess." I was going to go on about the possibility that she might have been the root cause of the charm, even though I knew deep down it was the whole Paul Levy murder.

But I had to exhaust all possible reasons for this.

"I love Oscar. I do. But I did tell you that you needed the ancestral dance at midnight to get the Good-Sider blessing." It was the *I told you so* moment Aunt Helena had been dying to give me since I said I do and had not given in to her and Eloise's ritual demands.

"It's not my marriage." I brushed the back of my hand along the bottom of my nose. "I . . .I'm a suspect in a murder."

"What? That is what you are accusing me of? You think I would murder someone and make it look like my own flesh and blood did it just so you wouldn't have a baby with a Dark-Sider?" Aunt Helena jerked back and drew her cloak up and over her shoulders. "That is a low blow."

"What, no! I don't think you murdered anyone! I'm just asking questions to figure out what in the heck is going on in my world. I'm just asking…" I held my hands out in front of me to try to defuse the electric energy between the two of us.

She glanced around before grabbing me by the arm. "Come with me."

I did what she was told me to do. I had nothing better to do and if she could shed some light, I was in no position to not listen.

She dragged me through the café and out into the street. She hurried me down the sidewalk, across a pathway that led to the small yellow cottage that had window boxes under each window overflowing with geraniums, morning glories, petunias, moon flowers, and trailing ivy leaving a rainbow of colorful explosion. The awning flapping in the chilly breeze read Intuition School in lime green calligraphy.

The small schoolhouse brought back fond memories of when I first learned of my spiritual gift and how to use it. I tried to bottle that feeling and hold deep inside the pain I was feeling.

Aunt Helena flipped on the lights, illuminating the interior filled with a few rows of tables and a couple stools per table. I ran my hand over the front table where I used to sit. It was here that I had met Faith and Raven Mortimer.

"Raven," I gasped. My body shook with the feelings I had while I was deep in my nightmare and dismissing Raven as she held the ball of dough up in her fist exactly as she had done yesterday before I ran to The Gathering Rock and this nightmare started.

"Do you remember something?" Aunt Helena swept up next to me.

"I think I need to see Raven." My gut told me my words were right. "Before I rushed to The Gathering Rock to give baby Orin back to Petunia, Raven tried to stop me." I ran my hand over my wrist and touched my brass bell charm.

"Back up." Aunt Helena pulled out a stool, pointing for me to sit. She pulled up the other one and sat down, facing me. "I'm not following you."

Quickly I filled Aunt Helena in on what had happened—all the details of Paul Levy, why I was at Hidden Halls, and I also gave her insight on my nightmare.

"Then you must see Raven. And visit everyone who was in your nightmare. They hold the answers to all the questions surrounding the death of this man." Aunt Helena confirmed what I had felt. "She might have some insight." Her eyes drew down to my wrist. "Brass bell?" Aunt Helena asked with a frosty tone.

"Yes," I answered bleakly.

"And you got this before you chased after Mr. Levy?" Aunt Helena asked with a condescending inflection.

"I know. I know." I shook my head in shame.

"You've got to start listening to your familiars." Aunt Helena's brows rose.

"Yes she does!" Madame Torres chirped from the bag.

"Starting with her!" Aunt Helena pointed to my bag.

"And that is easier said than done." I pulled Madame Torres out of my bag and sat her on top of the desk.

"I understand that, but you have to listen to them and your night-mares. They are part of what makes you and creates your spiritual gift. These are what make you who you are. Good or bad," she said and got up from the stool. She circled around the room gathering all sorts of items before she proceeded to the front of the room where she kept a cauldron. She flipped it on and sprayed a few spritz of the cauldron cleaner in it before wiping it out.

Intuition class was really fun. Aunt Helena put together all sorts of potions and the students used their intuition along with their senses to figure out who or why someone would need that potion.

"I have no idea who Paul Levy even is." I shrugged. "But I do know that I need to see Raven and find out where this carnival travels from. Maybe there is something in his past that will connect me to something."

Unfortunately I was afraid the train was the link and I knew it deep in my gut.

Madame Torres swirled and twirled, sending her face off into a tornado inside her crystal ball. The blue and purple swirled into a black cloud mixed with flecks of gold turning into a sea of silver. The storm inside her ball calmed to a slight wave.

Students filed into the cottage one-by-one, filling the stools. I didn't bother paying attention to who sat next to me because I was too busy watching Madame Torres's calm wavy sea turn into a roaring choo-choo train. The same roaring the train had in my nightmare.

"June." The tone in Aunt Helena's voice was not pleasant. Sort of unhappy, to say the least. "You have to pay attention in class." She swept from one side of the schoolhouse to the other in a fluid motion, her red cloak swept the floor behind her. "How can you learn anything new if you keep daydreaming."

"I wasn't daydreaming." The images of Madame Torres continued to play over in my head. The only choo-choo I had ever seen that looked like that one was when I had to go to Azarcabam. A place I didn't intend to visit in this life again.

"Then what do you call this?" She stopped, put her hands under her chin and let her eyes focus off into space. "That was how you looked."

"I was listening to my intuition like you told me to do." I grinned and ran my hand over Madame Torres. "I think I just might know who I need to see about Paul Levy."

"Using your familiar is the ticket to success." She snapped her fingers.

"Ticket," I groaned. "If you only knew how much I didn't like that word."

The last thing I wanted was a ticket to Azarcabam. The last time I had gone there, I had been jailed and Mr. Prince Charming helped me dig my way out. It wasn't a place to visit for the fun of it or for vacation. It certainly wasn't somewhere I wanted to go for a honeymoon.

CHAPTER THIRTEEN

H ow could I not have thought about this before? I questioned myself on my way back from my class.

Aunt Helena and I had said our goodbyes with a promise from her that she would help me in any way she could. Aunt Helena had powers beyond I could ever imagine. I'd put money on it that she was busying herself right now with trying to figure out who Paul Levy was.

When she accused me of daydreaming, there was no way I was going to tell her about what had actually popped into my head. Eloise Sandlewood.

The clinking sounds of the chains from the incense burner Eloise was swinging back and forth gonged in my head along with images of her lips as she cleansed Magical Moments.

I stopped at the wheat field before I reached the sign pointing the direction back to Whispering Falls.

Mr. Prince Charming turned and looked at me before he sat down facing the way home. I reached in my bag and took out Madame Torres. I held her up to my face.

With my other hand, I slowly rolled my hand over her. It was time to get some much needed answers away from the other people in my life. And my intuition took over as I let my hand float without thinking.

"I see the waves of water. I see enlightenment that is going to provide me answers that I need. I see a gifted person with keen logic and natural intuition, giving me insight my intuition will not allow," the words flowed out of my mouth as Madame Torres took over my voice. "This person will have a great influence on your present situation. To get to the heart of the matter, the person is the key to the answers you seek. The poisoned one was going to help you. He had a message for you. He was stopped. The evil has taken over." The words continued to come out. The waves disappeared and the train appeared. "Have a wonderful day, blessed be."

Just like that, Madame Torres's ball went black.

A jolt to my core caused me to step back. I gripped Madame Torres and sucked in a deep breath of fresh air, filling my lungs as much as I could and slowly releasing through my mouth.

Meow. Mr. Prince Charming sat down at my feet and looked up.

"I'm fine." I shook my head and put Madame Torres back in my bag. "That was a new one."

Over the past couple of years Madame Torres showed me things, but nothing where her words took over my voice and I had no control over it. When I had come to Whispering Falls and found out I was a witch, Izzy told me that over time my gifts would sharpen. It was definitely time to stop by and see her. But the first person on my list was Eloise.

I touched the wooden arm that read Whispering Falls. Stalk by stalk, the wheat began to disappear. Vibrant pink Iceland poppy jumped out of the earth followed by complimentary fuchsia ground cover erica. With each step I took closer to home, a new fall and winter flower or ground cover paved my way. Yellow English primrose, yellow winter jasmine, snap dragons, and purple ornamental kale to name a few. All the colors created a beautiful picture around me and Mr. Prince Charming. The aromas helped clear my soul and add just enough positive intuition that I began to feel better about my situation.

If I listened to Madame Torres, there was someone out there who wanted to help me besides Paul Levy since Paul wasn't going to tell me anything now. Who was that? The poisoned one Madame Torres talked about was Paul. What did Paul try to save me from? Who was he saving me from?

All of these questions rolled around my head. Mr. Prince Charming was probably already halfway down the hill to Whispering Falls by the time I made it to the wooden sign at the end of the path. The sign read: Welcome to Whispering Falls, a magical village.

When I passed the sign, I turned around and all the colorful flowers were gone. It was just the wheat field. I took a sharp right and walked deeper into the woods on my way to Eloise's house.

Whispering Falls was originally a Good-Sider community, which meant any Dark-Sider had to live on the village outskirts. When I was village president, I merged both worlds and now Dark-Siders could come and go as they pleased. But Eloise continued to live in her home in the woods. And I didn't blame her.

Not only did she have plenty of land for her herb garden, she was surrounded by beautiful nature and peace that no village, no matter how small, could give her.

Most days I found Eloise's house a nice getaway, but today I needed answers.

The mid-afternoon sun shone between the two trees, exposing the two-story house built on a platform high off the ground. A set of wooden stairs led up to her cozy wrap around porch where Oscar and I loved to enjoy our after dinner tea when she had us over for dinner.

I walked around the side and noticed the lanterns that hung from the trees were still lit. It was strange since it was daylight. Still, I followed the lanterns to the gravel pathway where I could hear the drowsy daisy flowers humming along with the chilly wind. Along the path leading to Eloise's garden were beautiful flowers planted on both sides with pops of vibrant purple, green, red, orange, and yellow flowers. Wisteria vines provided a canopy leading to Eloise's exquisite garden. Rows and rows of herbs were neatly planted and proportioned perfectly with small wooden signs naming the herbs.

Mandrake flowers, rose petals, moonflower, mandrake root,

seaweed, shrinking violet, dream dust, fairy dust, magic peanut, lucky clover, steal rose, and Spooky shroom were just a few she had planted.

"Eloise?" I called when I made it to the end of the mandrake root row and saw the top of her head.

"June!" She popped up. There was some dirt smeared on her cheeks and nose. "I've got to get these shrinking violet bulbs pulled up before it snows even more." She stood up with a small purplish ball with dangling roots in her hand. She tossed it into a bucket, and then brushed her hands off on the apron tied around her waist. "What do I owe the pleasure?"

"It's probably not as much of a pleasure as I'd wish." I tried to smile, but the edges of my lips just weren't going to cooperate.

"Oh, dear." She came closer. "That doesn't sound so good. Is my nephew okay?"

"Perfect." Now that did make me smile. "I guess you haven't heard that a member of the traveling carnival for the winter bazaar has been found dead."

"Oh my. That is awful." She gestured toward the gazebo at the edge of the garden. I followed behind her. "I had no idea there was a carnival joining the bazaar. A death sure does put a damper on things."

"Damper?" I wish it were just a damper. "I'm the number one suspect and under village arrest."

"Suspect?" she questioned. Her back was to me as she stood next to the table under the gazebo. The table held two three-tiered stands. Each plate had a different pastry on them.

I reached around her and picked out one that looked like a pumpkin spice cupcake. I glanced over at Eloise. Her eyes were staring and blank, her fingers fiddled with each other.

"I saw you doing an extra cleanse in front of Magical Moments?" I took a bite of the cupcake. "I mean." I took another bite and mumbled, "Madame Torres keeps showing me a train. The last time and only time I was on a train was when Arabella Paxton moved to town and her father, Gerald, was trying to marry Petunia, only he was still married to Ezmeralda, who happened to put a spell. . ."

"I remember." Eloise stopped me and put her hand in the air.

"So you knew something was going on with Arabella and you didn't tell me?" I asked and casually poured myself a cup of hot tea.

"I had no idea you were involved." She eased herself into the chair. Her face was blank. "My incense does its thing. I'm chained to it. Not the other way around."

"Well, you can tell me now." I sat across from her in the other café chair.

"I had this interaction with a yellow ball during the Two Sisters and a Funeral cleanse. The wind carried the ball to Magical Moments. It was a sign." She drummed her fingers on the table. "I had no inkling of a clue A Charming Cure or you were in need of a cleanse."

Raven, the yellow ball, Paul Levy… all definitely had a connection.

The train.

I gulped. The train was the connection between the two worlds of good and evil. Evil would win if I didn't take matters into my own hands.

"I'm in need of more than a cleanse." I wished it were that easy. My intuition told me I was going to have to get to the root of the issue before I could even begin to have another suspect. "Did the wind tell you anything else?"

Eloise might believe the wind sent the little yellow ball, when I knew it was the ghost boy. Was he just playing with Eloise? Why would he still be bothering her after I had made it clear the night of my wedding for him to stay away from her.

"All I do is listen to the wind. I don't try to read into the spiritualist part because of the pesky law." Eloise had always played by the spiritual rules and still living on the edge of the woods proved it. "And now I wished I'd put a little more into the process since you are. . ." She teared.

I reached over and placed my hand on top of hers. Her fingers stopped drumming. Her emerald eyes slid up to mine.

"I bet Oscar is fit to be tied with me." Eloise withdrew her hand from underneath mine and wrung them together.

"Oscar doesn't know." I bit my lip and took a drink of my tea, staring into the cup to avoid any type of eye contact with her.

"June Heal!" Eloise's voice escalated, forcing me to look up at her. "You are his wife. I understood when things got a little hairy and you kept things from him before you said I do, but not now."

"He can't know that I'm taking things into my own hands," I protested. "In fact, the lawyer for Paul Levy is making me go back to intuition class. Can you believe that?" I asked and sat back in my chair.

"Did you say Paul Levy?" The look of fear struck deep in Eloise's eyes.

"I did," I confirmed. My intuition didn't need to tell me that Eloise had heard of Mr. Levy before. Her reaction told me. "Do you know him?" I asked and sat straight up.

"In a former life." She gulped. Tears sat on the edge of her eyes. "Did you say he is. . .gone?"

"Gone?" I asked wondering if she didn't hear I had said murdered. Dead.

"As in no longer living?" Her words came out as though each one was a little bee and stung her lips as it passed.

I simply nodded my head. The pain of my simple nod stabbed her. She curled her body over the table and rested her head on the edge. Softly, her shoulders moved up and down, a small whimper escaped her.

"I'm sorry," I whispered, though I did not know what I was sorry for. As far as Paul Levy was concerned, I was angry with him for coming into the shop and letting me believe he was a mortal by not identifying himself. "How did you know him?"

I figured it was better for her to talk about it instead of keeping her sadness bottled up.

"We were once engaged."

"Engaged?" I asked, stunned. "But I thought. . ."

"You thought I lived here all my life. In the woods. Alone." Her eyes softened. The edges dipped down. "You only know me from what you remember as a child and from what I've told you about Darla. But I did have a life before." Her words faded.

"The Parks?" It was like I could see it. "You didn't live here until Oscar was orphaned and sent to live with Jordan?"

Oscar's parents were murdered and he was sent to live with his uncle Jordan in Locust Grove, but this was before my father had been killed. Oscar and Jordan lived in Locust Grove before Darla and I moved there.

"You had a life but you moved here to be near Oscar." I knew my words were right. They came out of me like a fountain.

"Yes. Paul didn't want to leave Azarcabam and the comforts of the Dark-Sider life. He didn't want to be an outsider of Whispering Falls." Images of the two of them together formed in my mind. "I didn't blame him. What would he have done? Sat around here and tended my herb garden?"

"The train." My mind reeled with the images of Madame Torres. "I think the answers I'm seeking are in Azarcabam."

"You can't go there," Eloise voice boomed across the table, shaking it as though the earth quaked below us. "There has been such unrest since the last time you went. And I can only assume Paul left and joined the traveling carnival to get away."

"Didn't he know you were here?" I asked a simple question.

"Probably not." She stared down again. "I never told him goodbye. When we discussed taking in Oscar, it was just too much for him. He said he needed time and I understood that. It's hard for a man to take in someone else's child, but I thought he'd come around. Only I didn't want him to be forced to make the decision. So I took the train here and kept my distance. The rest is history."

"He did seem very interested in our wedding photo." I was beginning to remember what Paul and I had talked about. When Oscar and Colton had asked me about my conversation with Paul, I didn't think something like him noticing my wedding photo was a big deal. Turned out, it seemed like more of a big deal than I imagined. "The one with me, Oscar, Aunt Helena and you."

"Did he say anything?" she asked. Hope sat in her words.

"He just asked if you and Aunt Helena were our mothers. I told him you were the aunts." I smacked my hand on the table. "But he did ask where your husbands were."

"What did you say?" she asked as if we were teenagers sitting on the bed exchanging boy stories.

"I sorta said that the two of you were set in your ways and he laughed." I looked up at her. "Paul Levy was a very handsome man."

"Yes, he was." Eloise looked down. "I have a feeling there is more to why he was here than meets the eye if what you say about money and stress was true."

"You think someone saw him come into my shop or maybe someone in my shop was a spiritualist and knew I had made a potion for him?"

"And they had something against him and took the opportunity to frame you for it." She made a lot of sense. "But what was Paul into that would cause someone to want him dead?"

"That is the million dollar question." I sat back in the café chair and brought the teacup up to my lips. I knew Petunia Shrubwood held some of those answers. After all, it was she who insisted the carnival came to the winter bazaar.

CHAPTER FOURTEEN

There were so many people I needed to see. Petunia, Patience, and Raven were at the top. Narrowing down who was my first stop was a toss up since each of them seemed equally important.

But. . .I glanced down the hill over Whispering Falls. Dusk was quickly coming up on the village. My eyes slid toward Two Sisters and a Funeral, instantly I knew I had to get the Magical Cures Book.

"The ghost boy has been here a couple of months," I said to Mr. Prince Charming as though he was going to open his mouth and answer me back. I let my mind wander. "Strange things have happening since he's been here and that little yellow ball that he likes to play with keeps showing up in my nightmares and around my familiars." I ran my hand down my bag. "I can kill two birds with one stone." I smiled, knowing the two were connected. "Figuring out how to get the boy to the other side has to be connected with why Paul Levy was here. Plus if I get him to the other side, Patience will return to her normal self, making Constance happy."

Mr. Prince Charming did his signature figure eights around my ankles, letting me know I was on to something. It was like a puzzle. I knew I had most of the pieces, but how they fit together was an all-together different story.

The back door to A Charming Cure was unlocked and I had to slip in and get the Magical Cures Book if I was going to try to get to the root of Patience Karima's little ghost problem.

The little boy had shown up right before All Hallows Eve, long before Paul Levy came along. If I could find something out about the little ghost boy, I might have a clue as to why Paul was murdered.

The door opened into the back storage room that I used for storage and a little sitting room. Sometimes potions took longer than expected and I had a little sofa and refrigerator in there in case I had to stay later in the evening. I had stuck the Magical Cures Book under the couch one night when I was working on a new arthritis homeopathic cure.

Darla had always kept the journal next to her in the shed outside of our house in Locust Grove when she made her homeopathic cures. It wasn't until I had come to live in Whispering Falls did I realize the old tattered leather-bound book was actually the Magical Cures Book. Darla had written in the creases and around the pages and since she wasn't a spiritualist, the cures didn't talk to her like they did to me. She was keen enough to know that I would eventually need the journal for my future.

Mewl. Mr. Prince Charming appeared out of nowhere, nearly causing me to jump out of my own soul.

"You freaked me out," I whispered and shook my finger at him. I flipped the light on and walked over to the door. Faith was still in the shop. It sounded like she was cleaning up and refilling the shelves. It was closing time and I had limited time.

I rushed back over to the couch and bent down. Sticking my hand under, I felt around until I felt the leather-bound journal. I pulled it out, immediately put it in my bag and took Madame Torres out when she glowed.

I sat on the floor cross-legged and put her in front of me. I waved my hand over her and she appeared. The globe filled with purple smoke and yellow lines like static coursed through it.

Images of the brass bell charm Mr. Prince Charming had given me rocked back and forth in a rapid movement.

"Choooochoooooo," Madame Torres's ball chimed and the insides began to churn in irritation. "They seek you to finish out their evil! Turn to the water."

I watched in horror as the globe turned to dark blue waves, the bell gonging in the depths, a train coming right toward the angry sea that was alive in Madame Torres. The waves crashed against the globe. The storage room lights busted. Sparks flew. The train exploded inside of Madame Torres, the sea and waves calmed. The bell was still ringing slowing to a staccato back and forth.

The Magical Cures Book flew open. The pages were flipping so fast my bangs fluttered across my forehead. I steadied myself by placing my hands on the floor and waited for the flood of wind to pass. In an instance, everything fell silent and calm.

The book was open to a page that read in scrolling calligraphy, The Demons of Crimson. I placed my elbows on my knees and bent over the book.

This was how it worked. The book had a magical element I had discovered once I took possession as a spiritualist. When I needed a special ingredient or potion, I could count on the book to open to the right page. If a mortal outside of the spiritual world would pick up the Magical Cures Book, it would just look like a journal with Darla's handwriting. I read aloud, *"The Demons of Crimson will keep you or a loved one protected. The earthly possession is required in order for the protection to take place. Words from the tongue are not the cord to the protection, rather be thee must have a physical attraction that will bind until the earthly possession is complete."*

Madame Torres's insides twisted and turned in a fit of rage. The unsettled waves crashed and careened up against the glass ball. Train tracks appeared deep within the water as the lights of the train glowed bright, extending out of the ball and flooding the room. The sound of the train's horn echoed so loud I placed my hands over my ears and watched in horror as the train crashed at the edge of the ball into what looked like another big wave. Everything fell silent. Deafeningly silent. Darkness enveloped me. The sound of my breathing thundered in my ears. Even Mr. Prince Charming sat as still as a rock. Neither of us knew what had just happened or what that even meant.

"What on earth?" Faith stood at the door into the shop. The lights illuminated her silhouette. "June? Is that you?"

"It is." I grabbed Madame Torres and stuck her back in the bag. "I wanted to make sure you were okay."

"Really?" She flipped the light on and it flickered a moment. "You need new bulbs."

"I need a lot of stuff." I laughed. I ran my hand down my bag. "And I hope you keep this little incident between the two of us."

"Of course." She hurried over and put her arms around me. She gave me a big hug. "I do have to tell you something that I found very interesting today. It might help you."

"What?" I asked.

"Petunia came in here." Her eyes grew. "She was looking for a mojo bag for protection for babies."

"For Orin?" I asked and wondered why Petunia would need one.

"She said something about evil lurking. I asked her if it had to do with you and she wouldn't answer. And when I asked her if she wanted me to get you to make a special bag just for Orin she adamantly said no that she came in because she knew you weren't here." Faith's words went into my brain and stayed there.

I knew I had to analyze every word. But I knew the truth. Petunia was mad because I had Orin strapped on me when I came upon the dead Paul Levy. Not to mention Petunia had some very valuable information she was keeping to herself.

"I just found it odd that she needed a mojo bag for him." Faith turned when the bells over the front door clinked. "Oh," she put her hand out. "I better go lock the door."

I stood quiet, rubbing my hand down my bag. When my hand hovered over the Magical Cures Book, it warmed to the touch.

I crept over to the door into the shop and looked out the crack. It was Raven. She had two pink-and green-striped Wicked Good Bakery bags in her hand. The two sisters whispered between them. Raven's eyes looked at the storage room door. Faith must have told her I was there.

Raven's high-heeled black pointy boots clicked and she started walking toward the door. Her eyes tight with tension and a determined look on her face. I stepped away from the door, letting her come in.

"June." Raven took a deep breath, trying to relax. "I've been trying to get in touch with you all day."

"Please tell me you have a June's Gem in one of those." I really needed my tasty treat to help sooth my stress level.

"I have one, but it isn't good." Raven looked at me with an intense but secret expression. She handed me one of the bags filled with a handful of June's Gems. The other bag she kept clutched to her chest.

"Tell me." I begged to know. "I remember you trying to stop me yesterday, but I had baby Orin and he was so fussy. I just wanted to get him back to his mother."

Raven looked at Faith. Faith nodded. Raven opened the bag and pulled out a lump of beige dough. She slapped it on the coffee table in front of the couch and bent down. Her hands kneaded the dough. It looked exactly the same as Mr. Prince Charming when he sits on my lap and kneads my leg.

Raven had the ability to interpret and read signs left in dough or even in her mixing bowls. Her gift was Aleuromancy. She had seen many things in her dough since I'd known her and had been accurate each time.

She used her hands to spread the dough once she was satisfied. She used her finger to cut one inch around the edges. She picked it up and curled it in a ball. With a quick whip of her hand, she threw the ball down and it stayed in the perfect round shape. She picked it up again. This time throwing it harder on the table. Nothing. Then she threw it on top of the dough she had kneaded and flattened. The ball stayed in the round shape, but turned yellow.

Train tracks appeared in the dough and the ball rolled down it like it was a train. The ball stopped at the edge of the dough and the dough fluffed up into what looked like a wave on each side.

"There." Raven pointed. "What do you see?" she asked.

"I see a wave." Which wouldn't be too surprising since Madame Torres had been showing me waves.

"Come here." She pointed me to move my body to a different side of the table. "What do you see?"

"Oh my God," I gasped. It was like everything had been transformed. "Is that a mustache?"

"Yes. Just like the one Faith said Orin has." She looked up at me. Her brows drew in an agonizing expression. "As much as I want to say this had nothing to do with the man they found dead, I just can't rule it out."

"So are you telling me that Petunia knew this Paul?" I asked, keeping the yellow ball thing and how I already put two and two together that Paul was connected to Petunia to myself.

That was nothing new, but the why Paul and Petunia were connected was important. And that was what I hadn't figured out yet.

"Do you know how Paul and Petunia are connected?" I asked. Asking Raven was the most direct way to get the answer. I leaned over the dough and took a nice long look, hoping to see something like Raven, but all I saw was gooey, lumpy dough.

"I'm saying they are connected somehow, I'm just not sure how." Raven didn't offer me any solution. She pointed to the ball that was resting at the edge of the dough. "I do not know what this yellow ball of dough means, but I'm telling you to be careful."

I nodded. I did. It only confirmed that Patience's little ghost friend who had been here a couple of months was connected to this whole situation and somehow Paul.

"Well, I must go." She stood up and gathered all the dough into a big messy pile of goo before she stuck it back in the bag. "I have to get ready for the bazaar since I have now cleared my blocked mind by giving you this bit of information."

"Isn't it strange how magic can just block our minds?" Faith asked her sister.

"Hello?" I waved my hands in the air. "Did you forget that I'm the one on village arrest and the one who is being charged with murder?"

"I have no doubt this will all be cleared up." Faith nodded.

"I wouldn't be so sure." The negativity dripped out of Raven's mouth and onto my skin as if a snake were crawling all over me.

The extra mojo bags I had made up and stored caught my attention. One of them lit up like my ingredients for my potions did when I absolutely had to use one. Without question I walked over to the extra supplies and grabbed the cheesecloth bag I had made for a memory mojo. I stuck it deep in my bag, wondering what I would be using this particular memory mojo bag for.

CHAPTER FIFTEEN

There wasn't much sleep being had around my little cottage. Mr. Prince Charming couldn't get comfortable, not even with Oscar's side of the bed open since he was still on his twenty-four hour shift in Locust Grove. Even the inside of Madame Torres tossed and turned, creating lights around my bedroom.

Several times I had gotten out of bed and walked out the door to get in The Green Machine, my 1988 green El Camino, and zoom out of town toward Locust Grove, only I knew the Marys would get wind of it and then I'd never be able to figure out who really killed Paul.

Madame Torres chirped a message from Mac McGurtle that he wanted to see me for lunch and we could meet at The Gathering Grove today. I was sure he wanted to catch me up on the investigation in Paul's death and what to expect. I made a mental note to add him to my list of people to see. He should've been the most important, but he wasn't. Petunia was.

It was still dark out even though it was almost dawn. It was the perfect time to head down the hill to Whispering Falls and go unnoticed.

"Are you ready?" I asked Mr. Prince Charming and ran my hand over my charm bracelet before I grabbed my cloak and tossed it around my shoulders.

He danced in front of the door. I strapped my bag across my shoulder and out the door we went.

Petunia was sitting in the middle of the shop with Orin strapped around her while she did her ritual. She would sit on the floor and all the animals that lived in her shop would line up so she could brush them, give them a treat and get them ready for possible adoption. Only I had no idea who would want to adopt a squirrel.

There were so many questions I had for her, but not sure if it was the right time. She was probably still mad about Orin being strapped on me when I came across Paul. Still, I couldn't ignore the evidence presented to me. First the mustache on Orin was quite strange and the mustache along with the train in Raven's dough was something I just couldn't ignore. But the train was the most disturbing.

That same exact train was the one I had taken to Azarcabam and found out that Petunia's then husband-to-be, Gerald Regiula, was in fact from there and still married. Maybe Petunia didn't know everything that was going on, but I couldn't dismiss the fact that Orin had a mustache and The Demons of Crimson just so happened to do a protection spell but you had to have a physical scar until the deal was complete. Coincidence . . I didn't think so.

"Stop." I swatted away the group of fireflies that darted around my head, trying to distract me from looking into the window. Clyde, Petunia's pet macaw, lived in the display window. His head was tucked under his wing as he slept on his wooden tree perch. "Go bug someone else," I instructed the teenagers. "Or go on to bed. It's almost dawn." I was hoping to get them to leave me alone. Just like teenagers, they didn't listen to me.

In the spiritual world, your spirit could always come back in the form of an animal. I wasn't quite clear on how it all worked because it was Petunia's gift. She was an animal spiritualist. She could read them and helped lost souls become them. Fireflies were the perfect body for teenagers who have left the living. Like teenagers, they stayed up all night and slept all day. Plus they were always nosing around in my business, just like now.

"Seriously," I growled at them and batted my hand in the air. Mr. Prince Charming danced on his hind legs and swatted them with his front paws as if he were batting a string.

I looked back in the window.

"Crap," I groaned because Petunia was standing in the window, Clyde sitting on her shoulder. She stared back at me and wiggled her fingers in the air. She walked over to the front door and unlocked it.

"Good morning, June. I'm assuming you are here to see me." Petunia held the door for me to come in.

Clyde's beak was buried in her brown messy bun on her head. He pulled his head out and had a carrot stuck in his mouth. I should've been surprised to see a carrot come out of her hair, but I wasn't. There was an entire forest up there. The scary thing would be if she wore her hair down and brushed it. That would be something to see.

"I wanted to come by and check on Orin." I ran my hand down the book. For some reason I was needing some courage.

Instead of feeling the outer edges of a book, the crackle of the Wicked Good bag alerted my senses. I stuck my hand in my bag and pulled the sac of goodies out.

"I came with treats." I dangled the bag in front of her.

She smiled. She used one hand to take the bag and the other to rub on Orin.

"I am still mad that you. . ." She sucked in a deep breath.

"I did not kill that man." My brows rose.

She stuck her head out the door and past me. She turned it side-to-side.

"Get in here before someone sees you." She grabbed me and tugged me inside. She locked the door behind us and gestured for me to follow her to the corner of the shop where there was a real tree. She curled her hand in the air and suddenly we were surrounded by the light of the fireflies as they filled the branches of the tree.

"Um. . ." I looked around. I had never seen so many fireflies in one place. If they were alive and teenagers, it would be like I as at a rock concert surrounded by them. "What is going on?"

"They are on the lookout." She bit her lip and took out a June's Gem from the bag. She closed her eyes and chewed slow. "These do help melt the stress away."

"Why are they on the lookout?" My own stress level was rising. I grabbed for the bag and took a June's Gem.

"I've done a bad thing and I think the death of that man was because of me." Her eyes clouded with hazy sadness.

"What do you mean?" I asked and leaned a little closer. This could be the answer I needed. "It's important if it shows I didn't kill him." There was no way I was going to let her off the hook. I had come here for answers to why everything my familiar was telling me was pointing to this family.

"Well." She gulped. "Do you promise not to go nuts on me? I do have my baby here."

"Tell me." I could feel myself losing patience with her.

"A few weeks ago, Mr. Levy had come to the shop to see me. I thought he was here to look into purchasing a pet, but he wasn't. He was here to promote the carnival." Her words were chosen carefully. "It was very creepy."

"How so?" I encouraged her to continue.

"He said that he was happy to meet the village president and wanted to have his carnival here during our bazaar. I explained to him that the bazaar was just for our shops to be open and it was so cold that I'm sure rides wouldn't go over well with tourists. But he insisted they only did carnival acts like juggling. Having them would sweeten the pot, he told me that if I did approve the carnival, he'd make sure Orin was always protected throughout his life." She looked down at Orin. He was still asleep and snugged up against her. "You don't understand." Her eyes saddened. "Orin never sleeps. I'm so tired that I need to protect him from me."

"You?" I reached out and rubbed her arm. "You are a wonderful mother."

"No I'm not. Because." She looked up at me with veiled liquid eyes. "I let that man put a spell on Orin."

"Spell?" I asked knowing that the Demons of Crimson was exactly what Paul Levy had done to Orin.

"Yes. Some sort of promise that I would bring the carnival here in exchange for Orin's life-long protection, only Orin had to have a physical mark that would go away after I made good on my promise." She picked Orin up out of the snuggie and turned him toward me, adjusting him in her lap. "I agreed and Paul Levy put a mustache on my baby."

Everything that Madame Torres told me was right.

"What on earth did Gerald say?" I asked.

"He doesn't know," she whispered.

I jerked up. My eyes lowered. Had I heard her right?

"I'm sorry." I shook my head. There was no way I heard her right. "Did you say he doesn't know?"

"He does not. I just was so upset with no sleep that I had to do something to keep Orin safe from me." She cried. "He is sleeping now, but come in the middle of the night when I need sleep, he doesn't. Gerald doesn't seem to mind, but I'm losing my mind."

"Let me get this straight." All her words were up in my head and I had to straighten them out. "You're telling me that Paul Levy came to Whispering Falls to see if the carnival could come here for the bazaar. When you told him that we didn't use a carnival, he suddenly offered you this protection from yourself for your baby?"

"He said something about animals and how much love they can give and how we love them like our own children. It was then that I had confided in him about Orin not sleeping and I felt like I was going out of my mind." She sucked in her bottom lip, the edges turned down. "Then he told me about this protection and all I had to do was get the carnival here."

Something wasn't adding up.

"Why did he want the carnival here so bad?" I asked.

"He said that he and a bunch of other spiritualists had retired and were going around doing these carnivals. Their livelihood depended on it. He said that the extra work would help him connect with his child better. And since he understood how I felt, I trusted him," she said. "When I put it on the docket for the bazaar, I didn't realize I had to go through hoops from the Marys to get it approved."

"So that was why there was an emergency meeting?" Things were adding up layer by layer.

She slowly nodded her head.

The gnawing inside continued to eat at me. The more I thought about it, the more I truly believed Paul Levy was here on different business and it had to do with me. But what? I ran my hand around my wrist, feeling the brass bell charm.

"And now that he's dead, I don't think I will ever get this reversed." She ran her finger over Orin's manstache.

"And that's why you bought a mojo bag." Everything was suddenly becoming a little more clear on how Petunia and Paul were connected. "Paul is dead so your deal is null which means the protection is no longer in place and it means that the mojo bag is to help protect Orin from whatever evil lurked and killed Paul." My mouth dropped and my eyes slid toward Petunia. "Unless you killed Paul."

"Me?" Petunia screeched, offended.

"Yes. You." I got up and walked around the shop, talking out loud to myself. "You and Gerald are not sleeping. You aren't thinking correctly. Paul put this mustache on Orin, not only causing problems between you and Gerald, but making Orin the talk of the town." I drew my hand in the air and pointed at her. "Which you do not want people talking about your baby. What mother does?"

"June Heal, you have lost your mind!" She jumped up and fisted her hands. "Have you forgotten that it was your potion found on his lips? You were the one who broke the by-laws, not I!"

"You knew Paul was in my shop. I saw you looking when he left." My mind snapped back to seeing her in the street, watching as Paul left the shop. "It was perfect for you to set me up. Not that you wanted to, but your family is at stake." I twirled around. She was face-to-face with me. Her nose tipped up on the end. Her lips pinched together. "And that gives you the perfect set-up to frame me."

"I did no such thing." She spat. "What do you want from me to prove it?"

"I want you to answer some questions." I had Petunia right where I wanted her. My intuition told me she didn't have anything to do with Paul's death, but I knew she could help me.

"Fine." She crossed her arms across her chest. "What?" She sashayed back underneath the tree. I followed her.

"What does Gerald think about Orin and how he got it?" I asked. A leaf floated down from the tree. I looked up. Mr. Prince Charming was sitting on a branch next to a squirrel. I watched as the squirrel cracked a nut and held a piece out in its claw. Mr. Prince Charming ate it. The squirrel dropped the nutshell, barely missing Orin's head.

"He thinks it has to do with our heritage and maybe our DNA, you know kinda like the childhood illnesses the mortal children get, only this is in the spiritual world. And I just can't tell him that I put this curse on our child." She adjusted Orin in the crook of her crossed legs and picked up the nutshell. She inspected it and stuck it deep within her hair. "He forced me to take him to the doctor and everything. The doctor tested Orin for hormones and all sorts of stuff. They even asked if I knew anything and I said no. That was when Paul Levy was alive. I was sure the mustache would go away the first day of the bazaar when the carnival acts were walking around our street like Paul had promised."

"Paul Levy gave you a spell." I took out my Magical Cures Book and opened it to the Demons of Crimson page. I handed it to Petunia.

She lifted her hand and plunged it into her messy hair. She pulled out a pair of reader glasses and stuck them on the bridge of her nose. Her lips moved as she read the words printed on the page in front of her.

"This is not good." Fear hung on each word that left her mouth. She lifted her hand to her lips and used the other to rub on the kangaroo pack strapped to her as Orin wiggled a little. "I can't believe I did this to my baby," she cried out.

"It's going to be okay." My heart ached for her. I took her into my arms and let her silently cry. I rubbed her back. "I know you and I didn't kill him. Someone wanted him dead. He knew something and someone didn't want him to tell."

"What are we going to do?" she asked. "If anyone finds out what I've done, I will be banned as village president and worst of all, I have put my family in danger and Gerald will never forgive me for that."

"Still have the carnival at the bazaar," I suggested. I knew I had to travel to Azarcabam, but if I didn't find the answers I was hoping to find there, maybe the answers had to do with someone he dealt with in his carnival.

"I don't think so. Not without the Marys agreeing to it and without Paul Levy, who would I communicate with?" she asked a good question.

"I don't know. But I think I might be able to find out." I bit my lip. The words I was about to say made my stomach hurt. "You have to let me travel. You have to take me off of village arrest because I think I know where Paul is from and if I can go there, maybe I can find other people in the carnival."

"I don't know, June." Petunia shook her head. "I know that if the Marys found out I let you do that, I'd for sure be banned."

"You have no option," I reminded her. I tapped my finger on the Magical Cures Book to remind her of the Demons of Crimson deal she made with Paul.

"June Heal," she gasped and drew back. Her eyes lowered. "You are a very bad Good-Sider."

"No I'm not." I shook my head. "You are protecting your family and I'm protecting mine."

The words hung between us.

CHAPTER SIXTEEN

Petunia was hesitant to give me a leave pass from the village arrest and knew she'd receive some sort of discipline from the Marys for doing it, but she agreed. There obviously were no boundaries, and nothing Petunia wouldn't do for baby Orin.

We agreed that I would carry on today as if I were on village arrest and meet at midnight when the train for Azarcabam left the station.

My plan was to meet with Mac McGurtle at lunch. In the meantime, I was going to go back to see Patience. The yellow ball was vividly involved in my nightmare and familiars. I had to figure out how Paul and the yellow ball were related.

The street was filled with tourists shuffling in and out of the shops with heavy coats on. Today the snow had stopped, but the air was much colder. The wind had picked up and blew the snow from yesterday around in swirls and curls around the street, giving the illusion of a snowstorm.

I grabbed the edges of my cloak and tugged it around me, shielding me from the wind. I hurried up the steps of Two Sisters and a Funeral. Mr. Prince Charming batted the door, pushing it open a crack.

I pushed it open wider.

"Hello?" I called inside. "Patience? Constance?"

Constance hurried out of one of the rooms. She had on a plastic apron and goggles perched up on the top of her head. She peeled off the yellow plastic gloves and waved me in.

"Get in here before you let that cold in," she grumbled and headed back into the room from which she came.

I had been in that room once before and wasn't looking forward to going in there again. Clearly she wasn't going to come back out and talk to me, so I had to put my fear of looking at a dead body aside.

"Have you found out anything about my crazy sister?" Constance asked when I walked into the room.

The concrete floor had puddles of water on it near the drain underneath the steel table where one dead Paul Levy's body lay. Constance put the goggles back down on her face, making her eyes appear even larger than they already did in her thick glasses. She picked up some sort of hook tool on the metal tray and did some sort of poking and prodding to the body. I sorta felt sorry for him.

"Here he is." Constance continued to take samples from the body and stick them in little vials. "And if you think Patience is helping, you're nuts. She's out back playing with that ostrich." She lifted her hand and pointed the hook toward me. "I don't know if it's a good idea that you are here since he's here because of you."

"I didn't kill him." I glared at her, and kept my eye only on her. "You are going to figure out what did kill him. Right?"

"I'll move much quicker if you fix my sister." She threatened and glared back at me.

I walked over and looked at the clipboard on the counter with Paul's name on it.

"Don't be so nosy." Constance shuffled over and grabbed it. "His history is none of your business."

"How did you get it? Is there a next of kin listed?" This was all information I was sure I could use.

"You will have to fix my sister first to get this information." She hugged the file close to her body. Her eyes lowered.

"Fine." I jerked around and left the room. I didn't want to stay in there much longer anyway.

Mr. Prince Charming and I walked back out the front door and down the steps. The sounds of a hissing ostrich lead me straight to the back of the funeral home where Constance said Patience was.

Patience had on an orange cloak. Today her tight curls had little flowers stuck in them all over her head. The ostrich's neck flung forward as its beak plucked a flower from her. Her body shook like Jell-o as she giggled.

The yellow ball was near her feet.

"Patience." I smiled when I walked up.

"Oh, you." She rolled her eyes and turned away from me. "Do you have any answers yet?"

"No, but I think some answers are right here in the funeral home and I need you to get them for me." It wasn't going to be easy, but I had to bribe her. I pulled out the bag of June's Gems from my bag that was left over from yesterday and held it out in front of me. "I will give you these treats from Wicked Good if you find out who the next of kin is for Paul Levy. I need you to whisper it into the air so Madame Torres hears it and relays it to me."

"And you are going to give me those." Her hand reached out and she snatched the bag.

"And take you to get a caramel apple." I reminded her about the carnival. I so hoped they were going to have caramel apples.

"Fine." She tossed her head to the side. The ostrich jutted forward and grabbed another flower from her head. She giggled.

"I need to know if your little ghost friend has always had the yellow ball? Or did you have the yellow ball here?" I asked.

"It showed up the same day he showed up." She kicked the ball away from her foot, it rolled right back.

"Have you ever tried to take the ball away from him?" I asked.

"He gets mad. Kind of like at your wedding." She reminded me of his bad behavior that was not something I wanted to recreate.

"Patience! Patience! I need you to help me roll the body!" Constance screeched from the back door. Her eyes bugged out underneath the goggles.

"Roll the body." Patience's foot knocked the ball when she scurried off.

The ball rolled after her, but I stopped it with my foot when it tried to roll past me. I picked it up and gripped it in my fist.

"It looks like it's me and you," I said into the air.

Rowl! Rowl! Mr. Prince Charming hissed. The hair on his back stuck straight up and he darted off. His disapproval was apparent.

"You are going to go with me tonight." I stuck the ball in my bag and headed off in the direction of The Gathering Grove.

CHAPTER SEVENTEEN

The Gathering Grove had a line out the door when I got there. The knock on the front window caught my attention. Mac McGurtle had secured a two-top table right in front of the window just inside.

"June, how are you?" Gerald asked when I stepped through the door. He was cleaning off the table near the door. Two women were still sitting there.

"I'm good." I noticed he had picked up the teacup and slowly moved the cup in a circular motion. "I do want to ask you something."

Mac McGurtle lifted his hand in the air. I waved back to acknowledge him and gave him the pointer finger *I'll be right there* gesture.

"Mmhmmm?" Gerald's eye focused on the cup. He twirled a little faster. "Interesting." His brow cocked.

The two women were deep in conversation and didn't notice Gerald was using his gift to look into one of their futures.

"One second." He looked at me and bent down to the ladies. He said to the woman who looked to be in her fifties, "Can you please check your phone? I think someone is trying to get in touch with you."

She gave him a strange look. She put her hand on her cell phone that was face down on the table. She picked it up. There was nothing there, but a second later her phone chirped.

"Look there. There is a text message from my daughter." The woman quickly swiped her finger across the phone. As she read the text, her lips moved, and then curved into a smile. "She's pregnant! The medicine worked!" she told her friend.

"Congratulations." Gerald puffed up. "I just had my own child. Little boy."

"Congratulations to you." The woman gathered up her stuff. "We have to go. I have to go see them."

Before she left, she turned to Gerald.

"How did you know?" she asked, a curious look on her face. "I didn't tell anyone that my daughter was going to the doctor today to see if the medication the doctor had given her and my son-in-law worked. She hadn't texted me when you told me to check my phone."

"I have no clue." Gerald shrugged. He curled the edge of his mustache between his two fingers. "Here is a gift." He pulled out a couple of tea leaves from the front pocket of his Gathering Grove apron. "Be sure to have her steep these two leaves in hot water when you see her next. Let her enjoy a cup with a teaspoon of honey."

The woman's face was blank and slightly tilted to the side. Softly she said, "I will."

Her friend grabbed her arm and pulled her close, "I told you this town was magical."

They scurried out into the chilly day.

"Now what can I do for you?" He finally turned to me.

"Did you know Paul Levy before he approached Petunia to be part of the bazaar?" There was no sense in dancing around the question. I had little to no time.

"I did." His chin lowered, then lifted. "But I hadn't seen him for twenty years until he was at The Gathering Rock right before he was found dead in the woods."

"How did you know him?" I asked.

"He lived in Azarcabam when I did. I had left, as you know." He gestured around the tea shop.

"You didn't think to tell anyone that you knew him in the past?" I asked.

"Who would care? You were the one standing over him. Not I." He lowered his eyes down on me in an accusing way. "Besides, we never had a beef with each other."

"None?" I asked. He shook his head. "Then why didn't you think it was a good idea for his traveling carnival to come to the bazaar?" I tapped my finger to my temple. "I clearly recall you and Petunia standing right out there when I babysat Orin for you and you saying it wasn't a good idea."

"June Heal, are you accusing me of killing Paul Levy?" He drew his hand to his chest.

"I'm just trying to explore every possibility because I have no reason to want him dead. I didn't know him. I never met him a day in my life until he waltzed into my shop and disguised himself as a mortal. But you." I pointed to him. "You knew him in the past and you didn't want him here. That could be worth exploring." I asked, "Does Petunia know you knew Paul?"

"I. . .a. . ." He burst out in a cough. His jowls flapped back and forth.

I turned on my heels, leaving Gerald to think about what I was saying.

"Good afternoon," Mac harrumphed and greeted me when I made my way through the crowded café and sat down. He took his thick finger and pushed the glasses up on his nose. His blue eyes magnified.

"Good afternoon." I smiled and adjusted my seat closer to the table.

It was lovely to see the small vases on each table filled with Arabella's new holiday flower, Blood Mercy. Since Gerald was her father, she kept The Gathering Grove so vibrant with fresh flowers daily. I picked one out of the vase and stuck it in my hair. It made a very nice accessory on a dreary day.

"What was that about?" Mac asked nodding toward Gerald, who was rushing over to us.

"Hello. Hello." Gerald stood over us with a china teapot adorned with little rosettes all over it. He placed two saucers and teacups in front of us. "What can I get for you today?"

"I'll have the soup of the day." Mac pointed to the menu.

"I'll have the same," I said and took the strap of my bag over my head and hung it on the back of my chair.

Gerald lifted the teapot and poured the steaming tea into the cups. A few leaves fell from the pot. I lowered my eyes and looked in. Gerald's spiritual gift was a tealeaf reader and he was well known for being nosy. I wasn't so sure he wasn't trying to get a little reading off of Mac and me. After all, he probably wanted to know what I had up my sleeve with the information that he knew Paul before.

"I'll have some water." I looked up at him and pushed the teacup aside.

He hurried off in the direction of the counter that was backed up.

"You have him flustered." Mac smiled. "And if I know you, which I do, you know something."

"First you tell me what you know." I encouraged him. It was more important to me to see what he had uncovered in my defense.

"I am still waiting on the report back from the Karima sisters on the autopsy." Mac started out telling me something I already knew since I had just come from there.

I should probably let Mac know all that I have found out, but then he'd keep a close eye on me, hindering me from going to Azarcabam at midnight. And that was something I was determined to do.

"Well, I did find out something very interesting." It was a teaser for him to go and chase a lead that I knew was a dead end. "Paul Levy and Gerald knew each other years ago. I'm not sure if they were friends or not or how they knew each other, but they did. In fact, I knew Gerald was not happy Paul wanted the carnival to come to the bazaar and where I come from, if you are friends you want to help them in business. Not Gerald."

He gasped. His eyes grew even bigger under his thick glasses.

"How did you know this?" He grabbed his briefcase from the floor. It shook the table when he plopped it down between us.

"I asked him." It wasn't brain surgery. Mac looked over his glasses at me. "And Paul was engaged to Eloise."

"How do you know this?" he asked again. More dumbfounded than before.

"The morning of the murder, I saw Eloise give an extra cleanse to the village." I conveniently left out the part that tied Magical Moments with Azarcabam. Not that Magical Moments was involved with Paul's murder, but that was how the spiritual world worked. We got clues and we had to put them together, which led me to Eloise and the tie between the two worlds. "I couldn't help but go and ask her about it after I had been put on village arrest."

"Any clues on why she did the extra cleanse?" he asked.

"No. She said that she was just the vessel for the incense and wind to do her spiritual job." I sucked in a deep breath and hoped Mac would take my lead and run with it, ignoring me for the rest of the day. "She had no idea about the murder and when I told her and said his name, she became very pale and that was when she told me about her past with him."

"This is very interesting." He looked up at me before he bent his head back down to the folder he pulled out of the briefcase and began writing down what I was saying.

"I also remembered something." I stopped talking when Gerald came over and put the soup down in front of us along with my glass of water. When he left, I said, "When Paul was in the shop, I found him looking at my wedding photo. He did ask about Eloise and if she was a mother to Oscar or me. I told him who she was and he seemed to be taken aback."

He scribbled faster and faster. I didn't tell him about how I watched Paul leave and the interchange between him and Petunia. I needed Petunia's story all to myself because I had to keep her close to me, at least until midnight.

"I know you don't want to believe Eloise could do any harm, but the facts remain." Mac put the folder aside and picked up the spoon in his soup. He took a couple of sips. "Dark-Siders are from an evil side. If this

Paul was a Dark-Sider and had a tie here, maybe he was here to see her. And maybe they had an exchange in the woods, where Dark-Siders mainly live and she accidently killed him."

"Oh, no." I shook my head. This was not going as planned. I didn't want Eloise to be charged with murder. I only wanted Mac to research the lead of Paul and Eloise until I could get some solid answers without him on my back. "I think maybe she can give some insight to who he is. I don't think he knew she was here until he saw the photo of my wedding."

I did the best I could to get Mac to buy into the fact that he needed to stop watching me and focus on other possibilities.

"This definitely needs to be given to Colton and looked into." Mac slurped his soup. "I'll leave Oscar out of this since it's his aunt." He took another slurp before jumping up.

"Wait." I stood up, knocking my chair over. My bag skidded across the floor. "I didn't say she needs to be looked into by the police."

"Are you kidding me?" Madame Torres's voice was a high-sonic stiletto only I could hear. "If you don't get this crazy yellow ball out of your purse, it's going to drag me all over this village!"

My mind was jumbled trying to get Mac and my bag to stop, both going in different directions.

"Stop it!" Madame Torres yelled. "Stop bumping into me!"

"Mac!" I screamed out. The entire café fell silent. All eyes were on me.

At least Mac stopped shy of the door.

"*Ahem,* are you okay, June?" Gerald cleared his throat. His lips tipped into a nervous smile.

Our eyes met for a split second. My bag dragged across the floor. A collective gasp blanketed the café.

"I told you this village was magical," the woman next to me whispered to her friend.

"Magical?" I tried to play it off. "Oh no." I shook my head and giggled nervously before running over to the bag, stomping my foot on the strap. I bent down, picked it up and stuck my hand inside, pulling out the ball, but first noticing Madame Torres was lit up with words.

"I dropped my bag and the ball just kept rolling." I held it up in the air for everyone to see. "No magic here."

With bag and ball in hand, I turned around to confront Mac. He was gone. The door left slightly ajar.

"What can I get you?" Gerald's voice broke the silence of the café.

I looked at him. Gave him a weak smile and took a deep breath of appreciation.

"Look!" The woman who had whispered to her friend pointed at me.

The ball exploded out of my hand and shot out the door like a rocket.

CHAPTER EIGHTEEN

"Get back here!" I darted in and out of the crowded streets after the bouncing ball. "I'm not kidding!"

The ball bounced here, there and everywhere. There was no doubt in my mind that the little ghost boy had come into The Gathering Grove and taken the ball. Out of thin air, it was gone. The ball was no longer in my sight.

"Dang." I ran my hand through my hair, my eyes darted back and forth taking another look.

"June?" The high voice of Ophelia Biblio caught my attention when she said my name. Her curly honey colored hair cascaded down her back, giving me hair envy.

She stood on the steps of Ever After Books with winter garland in her hands that she twisted around the wrought iron railing on each side leading up to the bookstore. On each step, there was a three-foot tall nutcracker. Instead of them holding a rifle, they were all holding holiday-themed books. My favorite was a Buckingham Palace Royal Guard holding Charles Dickens's "A Christmas Carol".

"Are you okay? I mean. . ." She gave a sympathetic smile. The khaki awing with Ever After Books written in purple flapped from the wind above her head. The khaki color reminded me of Paul Levy's pants and Ophelia reminded me of Colton.

"No." I shook my head and looked down at my cloak, wishing I had put on a different outfit. I was so eager to get out of the house to see Petunia, I had thrown on an old pair of jeans and black sweater with snow boots.

Ophelia had on a pair of skinny jeans tucked into a pair of knee-high low heel brown boots. Her red plaid waist length coat was form fitted to her figure by a matching tie around her waist.

"Why don't you come on in and let's talk." She set the garland in her hand down on the step and held her hand out to me.

"I do have plenty of time." I smiled and reached out, taking my friend's hand. "And I could use a girlfriend's ear."

"You know you have mine." We slowly walked up each step.

"You have really outdone yourself this year," I said, looking over her head. She was only five-five to my five-eight.

Ever After Books was one of the most popular shops in Whispering Falls. She catered to tourists of all ages. The bookstore even hosted book clubs from surrounding towns or just girlfriend get-togethers. Of course she had food that was catered from The Gathering Grove and Wicked Good.

"What is this?" I asked when I saw the note taped to the door that read CLOSED. It was the middle of the day and the day before the bazaar.

She put her hand on the door knob of the shop, before turning it, she said, "I'm so light on inventory, I had to put in a book order, so I decided to take the day to get the shop ready for the bazaar."

We stepped inside the shop and immediately I ducked to miss a flying book that grazed my shoulder. I was still not used to flying books no matter how magical the shop. Books swirled, dipped, and dove throughout the colorful shop. Each of them had their own colorful wings, creating a rainbow of colors throughout the shop. There was a lamppost at the beginning of each aisle that gave a spotlight to the bookshelves that were filled with books.

Big comfy couches with large fluffy pillows and baskets of snuggly blankets in all sorts of bright colors were in each corner of the shop, allowing the customers to sit and hang out and enjoy Ever After Books as long as they wished.

I followed her to the counter, making sure to keep an eye out for the flying books.

"Hear ye, hear ye," Faith Mortimer's voice swept across the airwaves as she delivered the Whispering Falls Gazette. *"We are excited to announce the traveling carnival will be here tomorrow to bring jugglers, carolers, carnival foods, balloon artists, and many more fun carnival acts to the bazaar. This ad was brought to you by Glorybee Pet Shop. Be sure to stop by for all your pet care needs and send your customers to Glorybee for a 5% discount during the bazaar."* "Jingle Bells" played into the air giving Faith a little time between headlines.

"That's new." Ophelia tapped her toe to the music.

I agreed, but what was more exciting, I was happy to hear Faith's news. This meant Petunia had listened to me and somehow gotten the carnival to still come. Who did she talk to? Obviously it wasn't Paul Levy.

"The Whispering Falls police department would like you to come forward if you had any contact or had even seen Paul Levy the day leading up to his murder. There is very little evidence of Mr. Levy's whereabouts and the police need your help. Please see Colton Lance if you saw Mr. Levy or had any sort of interactions with him during his brief time in the village. This was brought to you by the village council where they are keeping us safe and sound in our little magical town." Faith giggled before she signed off. *"Happy holiday bazaar! Let's get our magic on!"*

"That is why I'm not okay," I groaned and plopped down on one of the couches. Ophelia stayed behind the counter. She'd grab a book as it flew past her, log it and let go. The book went to the shelf it was supposed to go to.

Faith's message put my intuition on high alert. Even with Paul's death, evil still lurked in our village. I could feel the tug on my gut. When Faith said the carnival was still coming, I instantly felt dizzy. The evil was still barreling our way and it had to do with the carnival. It was more important than ever to get to Azarcabam and figure out what Paul Levy was doing in Whispering Falls.

"Colton did say that it didn't look good. But we know you." She looked up. "We know that you couldn't hurt a fly."

"Thanks, but Colton was right. The evidence points to me." I looked off in the distance. Two books were fighting for a prime spot on the front shelf.

"Stop it!" Ophelia clapped her hands together. I jumped. "You are books one and two in that series. Work it out!"

The books twirled around each other again before they finally took spots on the shelf.

"Watch out!" Ophelia blurted out in a half-giggle when a book in the shape of a ball whipped through the air. I ducked just in time for it to hit the back of the couch and land on the cushion next to me.

"That must be meant for you." She chuckled at my near-beheading book fiasco.

My heart beat so fast, I put my hand up to my chest to keep it from beating out, and with the other I reached over and grabbed the book. It wasn't a ball, it was in the shape of a globe.

"I'm not so sure it's for me." I pushed it to the side. "Why on earth do I need a globe book?"

"I don't know, but my books have a way of picking out their owners. So humor me and take it." She grinned.

"Fine." I stuck the book in my bag. "Your books are kinda crazy."

"They get so competitive." She shook her head and went back to logging the books flying around her. "Anyway, back to you and your little situation with Paul. Let Colton do his job. Other people had to see Paul Levy besides you and Petunia."

"Petunia?" I asked being nosy.

"Of course. She is the village president who called the meeting. He somehow had to see her. I told Colton there was more to the story than Paul Levy wanting to come to the bazaar. If that was the case and he was in charge of the carnival, they book months in advance, not days." She lifted her head. Her eyebrow cocked.

"Thank you!" I jumped up. "I've got to go."

"But. . ." Ophelia sputtered behind me. I didn't wait around to hear her finish that thought. There was no time to waste. There was no reason I couldn't try to summon the train immediately.

I ran down the steps of Ever After Books and took a left on the sidewalk toward Glorybee.

The pet store was probably a close second to Ever After. People loved books and animals. The store was busy with people feeding the animals in the tree.

"Squawk! Hi, June! Squawk." Clyde, the macaw, flapped past me landing on the tree branch next to Mr. Prince Charming.

Mewl, mewl. Mr. Prince Charming greeted me.

"June," Petunia greeted me with a very disciplined tone.

"Listen," I bent over and whispered, "I don't have time. I've got to get to the train right now."

"Now?" She grabbed me by the arm and dragged me behind the tree. "What do you mean now? I thought we said midnight when no one will see us."

"I understand that you have a lot to lose, but I do too and this investigation is going nowhere. If I don't hurry up, then Eloise, me and you are going to go to spiritual prison and that is not going to happen if I can help it."

"I don't know." Nervously she put her fingertips in her messy hair. "I just don't know if I can give you a pardon."

"Do you want to get divorced?" I threatened. "Do you want Orin to grow up without a mother?"

"June." Her face contorted. "Are you threatening me?"

"I'm not only threatening you, I'm threatening the village president." I knew it was a bold move, but something had to be done.

Mac was already on his way to see Eloise and I couldn't have her arrested. Colton was going to start looking into Petunia and not to mention anyone else coming forward that had seen Paul and Petunia together.

"Did you not hear the news?" I asked her.

"I don't subscribe anymore because if I'm sleeping, which is rare, then I don't want to be woken." Petunia crossed her arms. "Why?"

"Did you approve any sort of announcement for the Gazette?" I clearly remember hearing Faith say it was sponsored by the village council.

"I don't know." She brought her hand to her mouth. "Oh my God! Gerald had me sign a piece of paper, but I didn't read it because I was so tired."

"Well, you approved an ad for the Gazette asking anyone who saw Paul while he was here in Whispering Falls to come forward with any information or anyone they saw him interact with." I pointed to her. "I saw you two interacting in front of my shop when he left with his potion. I could easily say that you saw him in my shop and framed me. Or I can go to Azarcabam and try to find some answers to help us all."

"Fine," she grumbled and stuck her hand inside the cloak she was wearing and pulled out a scroll. "I was going to give it to you later." She jabbed it toward me.

I took it and without another word, I rushed out of her shop with Mr. Prince Charming on my heels up the hill toward the wheat field.

CHAPTER NINETEEN

The grey clouds hung over the village. The snow had begun to fall. It was fresh, puffy and lay clean on the wheat field.

Meow. Mr. Prince Charming's long white tail was like a finger and pointed to the wooden sign with the picture of a train.

"I guess we are going on another train ride." I reached out and tapped the arm. I held the scroll that gave me the temporary pardon and stuck it down in my bag. Madame Torres glowed. "Oh, no." I had forgotten Madame Torres had a message for me.

The inside of my bag chirped. My cell phone. I had completely forgotten about it. I reached in and took it out, forgetting about Madame Torres and read the text.

It was from Oscar.

Oscar: *How is your day? I'm thinking of you. I hope you are okay. Work is crazy here. Christmas shopper galore. I will be home tonight.*

"Tonight?" I gasped realizing his twenty-four hour shift would be over. Quickly I texted back.

Me: *Great. I'm helping Petunia feed her animals tonight. I'll be home after that.*

I sure wished I was going to be home. I wasn't planning on staying in Azarcabam like I had done a year or so ago. In the jail. I was planning on asking a few questions and getting out.

Oscar: *Love you! Don't worry. Colton has really got some good leads.*

Me: *I'm not worried. I love you.*

I flipped the phone shut and threw it back into my bag.

"We've got to hurry," I said to Mr. Prince Charming and smacked the finger again. The sky was not only grey, but we were losing daylight.

Like magic, the wheat field parted, exposing the old locomotive I had ridden on before.

"All aboard for Azarcabam!" The same conductor hung out of the engine window like he had done before.

Wooh, wooh! The train whistle screamed. Steam blew from underneath the big hunk of metal and the metal wheels come to a screeching halt.

"Here we go." Looking back, I took one long look over my shoulder. I closed my eyes and took a deep breath. The heavy stench of evil filled my lungs.

It was still around. I knew what I had to do.

Mr. Prince Charming and I climbed up the lit stairs and through the big heavy metal doors in the only passenger car attached to the engine.

Once I reached the top of the steps, I looked back again toward the wooden sign and the direction of Whispering Falls. There was a tug at my gut. There were answers to be found and Azarcabam was the only place I was going to get them.

The shrill noise of metal wheels turning to get us going grew as they turned on the tracks, picking up speed. Mr. Prince Charming and I took a seat on one of the two red velvet benches. Mr. Prince Charming wasted no time curling up then closed his eyes as our adventure was about to begin.

I rubbed my hand over each one of my charms, remembering all the protection I had surrounding me. And my familiars.

"Madame Torres." I suddenly remembered her glow. I reached in and pulled her out.

"It's about time. I'm glad you got it now before it was too late." She let the text from Patience scroll through her ball. "If you get me stuck in some thrift shop. . ."

"Shh." I was having a hard time concentrating on reading the note.

Paul Levy is divorced from Yancy Levy. She lives in Azarcabam. They have reached out to her as next of kin, but she has not responded. They have no children. Paul recently retired from owning a toyshop called Dots.

The ball went black.

"Dots." I confirmed. "I must find a shop called Dots."

As I put Madame Torres back in my bag, my hand grazed the globe book from Ever After Books, tickling my intuition.

"Hmm." I pulled out the book and looked at Mr. Prince Charming.

He pushed out his front legs into a long stretch and yawned. He sat up on his haunches and licked down his front legs, tapping the book before he pulled them back to stand up straight and tall.

"This book really picked me?" I cocked my head to the side giving Mr. Prince Charming a glare.

Mew. Mew. The sound was barely audible between the rattling of the benches and the clicking noise behind my head.

The mini tassels on the red velvet window shades clicked against the passenger car windows like the sound of poetic rain.

I peered outside at the particularly dreary scenery as it passed by. The large castle on a hill that was located in Azarcabam was off in the distance. I knew the dungeon there well. It was a place I was not going to be visiting on this trip.

Thoughts of Oscar and our new life filled my head. There was no time to daydream, I had to find that toyshop and find some answers.

The train picked up speed. The wheels beneath me shook the passenger train floor. The tassels swooshed back and forth.

I held on to the red velvet bench with one hand and opened the globe book with the other, turning to the contents page. It seemed like the logical place to start, but nothing was very logical in my world right now.

My finger drew down the page and I quickly read the words, trying to figure out what I was supposed to find. The places didn't read Kentucky, Alabama, or Tennessee. It was strange names I didn't recognize. Strange places I didn't recognize.

"Azarcabam." My finger stopped midway down the page and dragged across to see what page number. "Twenty."

I closed the cover again to take a closer look at the book and it was still a picture of a typical globe. Nothing special. The pages flipped beneath the pad of my finger, my eyes scanned the page numbers, stopping at page twenty.

My phone chirped from the bottom of my bag. Without looking, I was sure it was Oscar letting me know he was safe and sound in Locust Grove. Or he was probably bored and checking in.

Instead of looking, I decided to check out the Azarcabam map. I rubbed my hand over the map. Underneath my fingers the landscape became bumpy and three-dimensional. I couldn't help but smile. It was definitely a book to keep.

Ophelia was right. This book was meant for me. Dots Toyshop was on the far north side of the village and this map was going to get me in and out.

Suddenly everything stopped. The noise of the wheels, the tassels hitting the glass, the creak of the metal and Mr. Prince Charming's snoring.

I looked out the window again. It was pitch black. Exactly like I remembered it.

"Get out!" The gruff, not to mention scary, voice that I remembered from last time screamed. "I said get out!"

The heavy metal door flew open.

"I said get out of my house!" The gruff voice wasn't messing around. "Just like you did last time you were here."

The last time I was here, the train didn't stop at a train stop, it stopped in this guy's shed, exactly how it had today.

"I'm sorry." I shut the map book and stuck it under my arm. I threw my bag over my shoulder and stood up.

I walked down the steps with Mr. Prince Charming next to me. The guy wasn't as scary as he was the last time. "I have no idea why the train must stop here."

"Me either." The man lifted his hand, his beard was much longer than last time and he was much more humped over. "Go!"

The smoke flew up in the air along with the flames from the barrel fires where the same men in black cloaks, mustaches, top hats, and dark lined eyes stood around it like they did last time. They reminded me so much of Gerald.

"Well, well. It looks like you are back." One of them recognized me. "If it weren't for that white cat, I might not have had a greeting crew here to meet you."

"What do you want this time?" The man grinned, exposing his toothless gums.

"I'm here to look for a toyshop called Dots." There wasn't anyone better to ask than them.

"Dots, huh?" Another man took a long draw off his cigar and made an O with his mouth. He puffed out little dots in the air. The smoke lifted above his head and formed the word Dots.

"Yes." I confirmed and pointed toward town. "That way is north, right?" I asked, gripping the edges of the book. They knew I was some sort of spiritualist, but I wasn't so sure they were as welcoming here as Whispering Falls was to our tourists.

"Yep, but not sure if it's open." Another man stepped forward. He was younger than the others. "I heard the owner was murdered."

"Murdered?" another one of the men asked. "Paul Levy?"

"Yep." Another added. "Damn shame." He shook his head. Vigorously he rubbed his hands together, brought them to his mouth, and blew on them before sticking them in front of the barrel to warm. "Yancy was leaving him because he just couldn't get past their loss. I'd heard Paul had decided to get revenge."

"Revenge?" I asked.

All the men looked at me.

"I mean, I'm not sure if I should go to the toyshop if there is something evil lurking." I shrugged and looked down when I felt Mr.

Prince Charming batting my leg. "But I guess this is none of my business."

They continued to look at me.

"I will be on my way." I gave a slight wave. "I'll see ya."

The men turned back to the barrel and brought their hands in front of them and carried on their conversation without me eavesdropping.

Not only did I need to figure out something about Paul Levy, Yancy Levy was now on my list. What was the loss these men were talking about? And why was Paul seeking revenge?

There was nothing about him that told me he was looking for revenge. It was only money. Stress.

The streets of Azarcabam were filled with all sorts of merchants and their wooden buggy carts. They pushed their wares through the streets, screaming at people to get out of their way.

Mr. Prince Charming ran ahead. He stopped and looked back at me. When our eyes met, he turned the corner of the building and darted off, disappearing around it.

I hurried to follow him, sticking the book in my bag. When I turned the corner, there it was. A big clue. And I knew exactly what Paul Levy was doing in Whispering Falls.

CHAPTER TWENTY

Dots was a stand-alone shop. The outside of which looked like a mini-castle. The spires of the castle had yellow round balls on each tip with yellow and red flags sticking out of each ball. The flags waved high in the air. Dots was written in black inside a round yellow ball.

"Could it be?" I questioned, stopping in front of the shop to get my head on straight.

My intuition curled deep inside of my soul. The yellow balls, the little boy, the toy store and Paul Levy were all tied together. The ghost boy showed up in Whispering Falls a couple of months ago with a yellow ball. Then Paul Levy shows up.

"Petunia." I gasped, bringing my hands together. Images of me in Glorybee played in my head like a movie reel. Petunia's words haunted my soul.

She said that Paul Levy knew about how children kept us up at night. The ghost boy and Paul. . .no. . .I shook my head trying to get the thought out. Only it wouldn't leave.

The ghost boy had to be Paul Levy's son. He found the boy in Whispering Falls. And the boy. . .I snapped my fingers. The boy was drawn to Patience because she's a ghost whisperer and more child-like than

Constance, only neither Patience nor the boy knew how to get him to the other side.

But why the carnival? Why was Paul pushing for the carnival? And why did my intuition pick up on money? The stress signal was clear. But the money?

"Hello." The woman stood next to me. Her long black hair lay in waves down to her waist. Her long thin pale face made her black eyes and red lips pop. Her long eyelashes seemed to brush her cheeks. "Would you like to come in?"

"Yes." I knew she was Yancy. She didn't need to know why I was there. I already got the answers I was seeking and now I needed to go back to Patience and have her communicate with the boy. Maybe he had some answers about why Paul would have been murdered.

"Are you looking for something in particular?" she asked. Her long brown cloak swooshed behind her as she walked me up to the toyshop. It was embroidered with orange swirls and yellow dots. It was very lovely and she was even lovelier.

"I am looking for a plastic ball for a little boy." If I had to go in, I might as well try to get some more information about her.

"You are new to our Azarcabam?" she asked.

I followed her over the drawbridge of the pretend moat. I was totally envious. I had never seen a toyshop like this one.

"I'm passing through." I kept it as simple as possible.

The inside of the toyshop was amazing. There were three open floors of toys and displays as far as my eyes could see. The right side of the store was interactive. A few children and their parents were milling around. There was a Lego room where children were putting together their own designs. There was a water play area where children were scooping and pouring into different containers. The ball pit was filled with children diving into the squishy fun. Plus many more rooms I couldn't see.

"You have a very funny traveling companion." She gestured to Mr. Prince Charming who had found a nice spot in the middle of display of yellow balls.

"Yes I do." I smiled as my familiar confirmed to me that the ghost boy was in fact the son of Yancy and Paul Levy. "I guess I'll take one of those."

"You can never go wrong with a yellow ball." She woman picked up a ball from the pile and held it to her heart.

My head swam. I felt dizzy. My intuition engulfed my entire body. The grief of the woman overcame me. Tears dripped from my eyes.

"Are you okay?" she asked.

"Are you?" I asked back. Images of me and Darla rolled around me. Images that I had tucked deep inside my memory.

Darla, I don't want to leave. I want to stay here in Whispering Falls. My little hand reached up for my mother. *I know dear, but your father is no longer here and we need a fresh start.* Darla looked back and smiled. I looked back to see what she was smiling at. Eloise stood on the edge of the woods with her hands folded in front of her. *We are going to live in Locust Grove where you can go to school and play with other little girls your age.* She took my hand. *But I don't want to play with other little girls. I want to play with you and your lotions.* She tugged on my hand.

"I'm fine." Yancy brought me out of my memory.

There was a connection between my memory and . . .my mouth dropped. Yancy Levy was not a spiritualist and they were making her close shop like Whispering Falls had done to Darla after my spiritualist father had died.

"I'm in the process of moving and I hate to leave my shop." She held the ball closer to her chest. "I'm just thrilled you'd like a ball. My son loves. . ." She stopped and swallowed. "He loved to play with this particular brand."

"Loved?" I knew the answer but I didn't want to seem insensitive to her.

"Yes. My son had a terrible childhood illness that took his life a couple of years ago." She walked behind the counter and punched on the cash register.

"I'm so sorry for you and your husband's loss," I whispered, feeling a little guilty that I couldn't tell her that I'd been playing with her son.

"My husband never got over our son's illness or death. He sort of went a little crazy and was on a mission . . ." She bit her lip. Her black eyes riddled with sadness. "He divorced me and now he has been killed."

"Killed?" I asked, though I already knew.

"I'm so sorry." She smiled and handed me the ball. "I have no idea why I'm telling you all this. Take the ball for payment for being my therapist."

"Oh no." I dug deep in my bag to get some money. I pulled out the mojo bag that my intuition had told me to grab before I had left Whispering Falls. "Let me give you this."

I dangled the cheesecloth bag out in front of me.

"I am a homeopathic curest from Locust Grove, Kentucky and this is a mojo bag with some stress relief." I handed it to her. She took it. I clasped both my hands around hers. "I want you to take a bath tonight when you get home. Sprinkle the contents of the bag into the warm water, letting it dissolve completely. Take five deep breaths and then close your eyes. Do not close your eyes when you take the deep breaths. You will want to, but don't."

The bag was going to fill her spirit with happy memories of her child and her husband. It would help her move forward in her life and be able to move away from Azarcabam like Darla had done.

"Just talking to you makes me feel better somehow." A tear trickled down her face. "Please, take the ball."

"Thank you." I let go of her hands and took the ball from the counter, sticking it deep within my bag.

My phone chirped. I grabbed it and quickly looked.

Oscar: *June, I cannot believe you have put Petunia in this situation. I'm coming after you.*

Suddenly I felt sick.

CHAPTER TWENTY-ONE

There was no way I wanted Oscar to come get me. I had gotten the information I had come for and figured out why Paul had come to Whispering Falls. Well sort of. I knew he had come to find his little boy, but why was the carnival so important? Had someone promised him something if he did bring the carnival? What would that person want from Whispering Falls?

My gut told me that when Paul saw the photo of Eloise, he couldn't go through with whatever it was he was sent to do. Had this person promised him his son back?

All of these questions floated around in my head. Maybe my time in Azarcabam wasn't over. Maybe the answers to my questions were here.

I stepped out of the castle and stood on the drawbridge looking down the main street of Azarcabam. The old buildings were dark. I had been in a few of them before and I knew not to go back. There was an old saloon type bar down on the right.

Laughter spilled out into the streets followed by the tapping of tambourines. A group of fiddlers and women twirling around hooted and hollered, dancing in the street. The women's gold chains that hung around their necks glistened in the dark. The sound of their bangle bracelets jingled along with the clink of the tambourines.

They all had long brown hair that hung loosely in large curls around their colorful faces. The men in balloon pants stomped their bare feet on the ground as they yelled out and got down on their fiddles. The strings of the bow ran across the fiddle in a shrill tone as quickly as they could move their hands.

The women twirled around the fiddlers, kicking their legs in the air with each pat of their tambourines. They wore pink skirts and gold coin chains dangling from their waist and loose blowsy tops draped their top half.

They gave me shivers seeing them dance in the snow covered streets. I slipped out of sight and into the darkness to keep out of sight. My last interaction with them was not one to be repeated.

A hand grabbed my bicep and dragged me into one of the buildings. Another hand clamped around my mouth.

Mr. Prince Charming jumped into the air. His claws out, he grabbed onto the person behind me.

"Ouch!" The hand let go of me and the person stumbled backward. "I swear that cat hates me."

"Oscar?" My jaw dropped when I recognized him. Mr. Prince Charming sat at my feet. I swear he was smiling.

"I told you I was coming." He ran his hands down his legs and rubbed out the pain from Mr. Prince Charming's claws.

"You shouldn't have grabbed me like that." I wanted to laugh because I knew Mr. Prince Charming had wanted to attack Oscar for years, but never had the opportunity. "After all he is my familiar and part of his job is protecting me from people who want to grab me."

"I'm your husband." Oscar glared at Mr. Prince Charming. The two stared at each other.

"You shouldn't have come. I got what I needed and now I'm going back to Whispering Falls. No one knows so I'm fine." I grabbed him by the hand to get him out of there.

"No, it's not all fine." His words were sudden, raw, and angry. "Colton has been looking for you because Mac told him about Eloise's relationship with Paul Levy. He wanted to get some answers from you."

"Oh." This meant I was really in trouble for breaking my village arrest.

"So he went to the village president." His words stung me. "When he found that Petunia had given you immunity without clearing it with the Order of the Elders, he arrested her. The Marys showed up and took away her presidency and put her in jail until they find you."

"I. . ." I was speechless. I never figured my own lawyer would go to Colton. I figured Mac would go and check out the information, giving me time to get to Azarcabam and get the answers.

"That is the problem. I. I. I." He shook his head and headed down the back alley, keeping in the shadows. "When you get into a pickle, it's always 'I this, I that.' You never seem to think how your I's affect everyone around you."

Before I knew it, we were back at the shack. The train was waiting for us. As much as I wanted to tell Oscar what had happened while I was in Azarcabam and how I found out about Paul Levy's child, he was in no mood at this time. It would only make him mad. Plus I still didn't have the answer to why Paul was murdered. I only had the answers to the ghost boy and who he was, the yellow ball and where it had come from, and the fact that Paul put a spell on Orin that might not ever go away.

"You are going to go to jail now. I told them I would bring you in." Oscar sat on the velvet bench. Disappointment on his face. "You have to stay there until the bazaar is over."

"The bazaar!" I gasped. "But. . ."

"No buts." Oscar folded his arms across his chest, rested the back of his head on the glass of the passenger car and closed his eyes.

There was no reasoning with Oscar Park when he got mad. I had known this since we were children. He would get mad at me and not talk for days. Unfortunately for him, we were married now and he had to put up with me. Only, I knew he wouldn't listen to anything I had to say. I might have had some facts, but nothing got me out of murder.

Mr. Prince Charming was curled between us. The sound of the

tassels knocking against the glass was steady, like a white noise, putting me to sleep.

Come on, June! Darla's voice called between the sounds of ringing chimes and gonging bells.

I want a caramel apple. I pointed to the lady in the pointy hat walking around the carnival that had come to town. She had a sweet smile; her teeth were so white. I was eyeing the tray of apples on sticks that were neatly dripped in hardened caramel. My taste buds were watering.

You know you cannot have any sugary treats. Darla insisted I never eat the bad stuff, as she called it. That was where my addiction to Ding Dongs had begun. Oscar's uncle Jordan always bought those yummy treats and Oscar and I would eat an entire box sitting under the big tree in his front yard.

But it's a carnival. I really wanted one of those apples.

No. Darla wasn't budging. She bent down and looked at me. *You stay right here. I'm going to look at that booth.*

I watched as she walked off to look at some homeopathic booth.

Would you like an apple? The woman approached me. Her smile so inviting. *Go on, have one.* She shoved the tray in my face. My mouth watered even more. I reached out to grab the big stick attached to one.

No! Darla smacked my hand away from the tray. When I looked up to see the women's reaction, she was gone. Darla jerked my hand and without another word, she dragged me home.

"June?" Oscar shook me awake. "Did you just have another nightmare?"

I opened my eyes. The train had come to a stop and we were in the wheat field.

"No." I swallowed the dream. "More like a memory."

The mojo bag I had given to Yancy was probably for me, but it was too late. I had already given it to her.

"Memories?" Oscar looked concerned. He drew me close to him.

"Just memories of Darla." I let him snuggle me. I took a deep breath and let my body curl into his. Tomorrow I wouldn't be waking up next to him. I'd be waking up in the jail. Not where I wanted to wake up, but at least I knew I was safe there.

I shivered. The cold chill that had woken me up a couple of days ago had found its way back into my soul. This time my heart beat with fright. The evil was getting closer yet I was no closer to figuring out what was going on.

CHAPTER TWENTY-TWO

Whispering Falls was wide awake in the middle of the night. It was as if everyone had come out to see me being dragged off to jail. Animals from the woods were gathered outside, looking into the windows of the police station. The fireflies buzzed around, darting about in an angry fashion.

"June, we will figure this out." Izzy assured me when I walked into the police station. "We know you had good reason to leave."

"And I'll figure that out," Mac said. "Oscar."

"I hate this." He teared up. "You are my wife. This isn't right for me to be putting you in jail when I should be taking you home."

"Just as long as you know I didn't do it," I whispered and took a step forward to the steel door of the jail cell Colton was holding for me. I handed my bag to Oscar and he set it down on his desk.

The jail only had one cell in the back of the police station and I was happy to see Petunia was my roommate. She sat on one of the twin beds, cross-legged.

She didn't look at me. She kept her head down.

"Your animals are here to support you." I tried to make her feel better. Once everyone gave us peace, I'd tell her what I discovered in

Azarcabam, hoping she'd be able to help me shed some light on the situation.

She crossed her arms and turned toward the wall.

"I guess I have to go." Oscar's hands gripped the cell bars. Colton shut the door and locked it. "Good night, June. I love you."

"I love you." I smiled, trying to reassure him that everything was going to be okay.

Colton rushed everyone out but Mac.

"Tell me what this was all about?" Mac asked. His pen and paper at the ready.

"I'm tired." I pushed my hair out of my way. "I just want to go to bed." I sat down on the mattress. "Can't we do this tomorrow?"

"Tomorrow is the bazaar and there will be so many people in our village. It would be better to get your statement tonight," he said.

"There is no statement. I tricked Petunia into giving me immunity and I ran." I shrugged. "Plain and simple."

"I don't believe you." Colton stepped up to the cell. His blue eyes fell upon me. "I think you were trying to find something."

"Well, I didn't." I lay down on the bed and crossed my ankles and my arms. I closed my eyes.

It seemed like forever until Mac left us alone. Petunia was still silent.

"I'm going to go ask Eloise some questions. I'll be back." Colton looked at us. Petunia didn't move and neither did I. Though I did wonder why he couldn't wait until the morning to talk to Eloise.

When I heard him lock the police station door, I sat up.

"Petunia, I know you don't want to talk to me but you have to listen." It was time to tell her about my trip to Azarcabam and maybe get some insight from her.

She didn't move. She just stayed looking at the wall.

"Just listen." I sat on the edge of the bed. "I think I got some good stuff. Paul and his wife Yancy, his mortal wife," I emphasized mortal, "own a local toyshop in Azarcabam. Oh, you'd love it. It's this big castle with all sorts of. . ." I ran my hand over my face. "I'll stick to the facts."

She was obviously in no mood to hear about Dots.

"They had a son who died of a childhood illness. Paul was so grief stricken that he never got over it. Yancy is now having to move out of their village since he is no longer alive. Here is why he came to Whispering Falls." When I saw Petunia perk up a little, I continued because I knew she was listening. "You know that yellow ball that is all over town?"

She didn't budge.

"Well, that ball belongs to a little ghost boy that has been bugging Patience but not Constance. Constance insists that Patience is going nuts and giggling to herself, but the ghost boy is making Patience laugh. He is keeping her company. The boy," I sucked in a deep breath, "is Paul Levy's son."

"How do you know that?" Petunia jumped around. Her messy updo flipped to the right and then to the left. A bag of peanuts fell out. She reached down and picked them up, holding them out to me.

I took it as a peace offering and got up. I walked over to her bed and sat down.

"Dots, Paul's shop, is inspired by this yellow ball. They even sell them there." I pointed toward my bag. "I have one in there to show you. Yancy gave one to me."

"You told her?" Petunia face looked mortified.

"No." I assured her and took a handful of peanuts. "I gave her a mojo bag in exchange."

"How is this going to exactly help us?" she asked.

"Paul was obviously here to look for his son and someone has promised him something if he was to get the carnival here." I chewed on the peanuts as well as my words. "Paul saw my picture of Eloise on the wall of my shop when he came in there." I still couldn't reconcile the fact my intuition said he was surrounded by money and stress. "He couldn't go through with whatever that person wanted him to do in exchange. . ."

"For the life of his son." Petunia eyes lit up. "What on earth does bringing a carnival here have to do with all this?"

"That is the million dollar question. And one I don't have the answer for." I let out a heavy sigh. "Being in here isn't going to help us solve it either."

I looked out through the bars and out the window into the pitch-black darkness of Whispering Falls. Tomorrow the streets would be filled with tourists and a carnival. A carnival that held the answers I needed.

I shivered.

"Are you okay?" Petunia's tone was frosty.

"No." I shook my head. "I'm afraid if we don't get the answers soon, the evil is going to take over our village for good."

A cold draft swirled around us. Both of us shook.

CHAPTER TWENTY-THREE

S omething woke me up into my reality. Somewhere I didn't want to be. I glanced over and Petunia was asleep, curled on her side. Outside was half dark, half light. The silhouettes of Petunia's animals told me they were still outside waiting for her.

The day was beginning without me. I pulled the thin blanket up to my shoulders, trying to forget where I was. The sound of something dragging across the floor echoed inside of the police station.

I sat up. My bag was trying to get through the bars of the cell, but couldn't make it through.

"Get it." Petunia jumped to her feet and pointed to my bag.

"Good morning," I greeted her.

I did what she said and reached over. The bag jerked back, away from me out of reach. The yellow ball shot out like a cannon and bounced a few times.

"The boy is here," I said and watched as the ball bounced up and down in a rhythmic motion as though someone was bouncing it up and down. "Hi there," I said into the air.

Petunia looked at me as if I had lost my mind.

"I'm June with the cat. And I met your mommy." The ball stopped. It rolled toward the bars. "And I love your toyshop. I bet that was exciting growing up around." I walked closer to the ball. "Your mommy gave me this ball." I reached out to get the ball. It shot away and started to bounce again. "We," I gestured between Petunia and me, "need your help. I'm sure you saw your daddy at Patience's house."

I talked as though I knew what I was doing. Truth of the matter, I was not a ghost spiritualist and had no idea what I was doing. The ball stopped.

"I need you to go get Patience and tell her I need to talk to her. I can help you," I told him. The ball dropped to the ground. "Hello?" I asked. "Are you still here?"

"Great," Petunia's voice dripped with unhappiness. "You scared him off."

"I'm doing the best I can." I turned toward her.

"The best you can got my son and husband taken from me." She plopped back down on the bed. The door opened. Colton walked in.

"Good morning." Colton had his hands full of coffee and a bag from Wicked Good. "I come with food."

It was nice that Colton was trying to be kind to us, but that was not what we needed. We had to get out of there. He handed us each a coffee and the bag through the bars.

"Where did this come from?" he asked and picked up the ball. He also picked up my bag. "There wasn't any funny stuff going on here?"

"No." Petunia and I said together.

"Unfortunately, you two are going to have to hang out here while I walk around the bazaar and make sure everything is okay. I had to take Oscar off the case and told him not to come by until we get through the day." He put the ball and the bag back on his desk. "He said he'd work in your shop while Faith opened up Glorybee for you."

Petunia nodded. There wasn't anyone who could take care of her animals more than her.

"Not that your animals want to go back to the shop, but I've got to corral them if you can't get them to go back." Colton had warned.

Petunia threw her head back. Her mouth opened, "Mcbawk,

mabaw." Her head peaked the air. "Caw, caw, caw!" Her voice was shrill and loud.

The animals perked up, restless. Some pawed the window. But within minutes, they had left and made their way back to Glorybee.

"Thank you," Colton said.

"Did you go see Eloise?" I asked, curious.

"June, you need to worry about your case." Colton wasn't going to give me any information.

The stark reality was that I was on my own and dragging Petunia down with me. We sat there taking our time eating our breakfast and drinking our coffee in silence. The streets were filling up with people moving about. The shops had opened earlier with special hours and the carnival was doing exactly what Paul Levy said they would do.

There were balloon artists surrounded by children. There were jugglers keeping others entertained. The bazaar looked like it was going to be a success.

I was happy to see everyone enjoying the day, but itching to get out.

"Look at that." Petunia pointed to a little dog with a little coat on. It was on a leash and a family was walking him. "I bet they are going to my shop," her voice held sadness.

"I'm sorry," I apologized. Maybe it was time to give in. "I don't know where I went wrong. I'm sorry for bringing you down with me. I don't know how, but I will make this up to you."

She didn't look at me. She just laughed at the little dog, until her laughter stopped as if a valve shut it off.

"June," she gasped. She pointed.

My eyes drew down her arm and out the window where her finger was pointing.

Patience's ostrich was erratically running about, pecking anyone and everything it could. It grabbed the wreath off the carriage light outside of the police station. The wreath bounced in the air and like ring toss, landed around the ostrich's neck. The yellow ball was sitting as still as could be on the back of the ostrich.

"The boy's spirit," Petunia's words were haunting. "He wants to come back as the ostrich."

My mouth dropped. I had it all wrong.

"The ostrich is fighting the boy's spirit. It's confused and doesn't understand." Petunia stood up and closed her eyes. She lifted her hands out in front of her. "Mawbaw, chrickta, swignamba," she chanted out into the air. Her head lifted back, the chanting got louder.

My eyes scanned between her and the unruly ostrich. The ostrich calmed. Its neck craned to look into the window. The ball Yancy had given me started to bounce.

"If you would like me to help you become the ostrich, you must help us." Petunia brought her hands together. Her words were barely audible. "Get the keys and kick them in here."

The keys lifted off of Oscar's desk and slid across the floor.

"Good boy." Petunia chest heaved up when she took a deep breath. She looked over at me and smiled. "You had it all wrong. This boy has been here to come back in the spirit of the ostrich. Not here to play with Patience. The ostrich is just like a child. Runs around, doesn't listen, likes to play." She smiled. "Now we have keys to get out."

"You don't have to do this," I said. "You can stay here and I'll tell them that I blackmailed you. You need to go back to your family. Baby Orin needs you."

"Whispering Falls needs you, June." She bent down and took the keys. She reached around the bars and unlocked the cell door, flinging it open. "Let's go."

CHAPTER TWENTY-FOUR

Instead of going out the front door, we headed out the back, but not without me taking Oscar's Whispering Falls police uniform and putting it on. Petunia was going to slip out into the woods. The animals would keep her safe until I figured out what evil was lurking in the carnival.

I made my way behind the shops and walked between The Gathering Grove and Mystic Lights. Patience was standing in the middle of the street looking down and then up.

"Get back here!" she screamed as the ostrich ran past her. The ball was still on the back of the creature.

I took a step out to the street when a carnival worker stepped up and stopped Patience.

"I know you would like a nice warm, caramel apple." The hand of the carnival worker was that of a woman.

Patience smiled and clapped her hands together.

"My friend, June, was going to get me one, but I'll take yours." Patience's hand lifted to get an apple.

Panic welled in my throat. As the images of me and Darla at the carnival in Locust Grove focused into my memory, a terrifying realization washed over me. The woman holding the apples was the same woman who tried to give one to me as a child.

"No!" I ran up to them and smacked Patience's hand away.

"June Heal." The woman's red lips curled up on the ends. Evil exuded from her entire body. The darkest laughter soaked the air around us. The woman's clothes turned into a cloak and veil. A black onyx jewel dangled down on her forehead. "I warned you that I'd be back."

She drew the cloak around her and a flash of light and thunder sent me falling to the ground.

"Ezmeralda." I leaned on my arm and looked up. She was gone. "My bag!"

I jumped up, bumping into the crazy ostrich. Stumbling up the street and into the police station.

Ezmeralda was behind this and there was only one thing she wanted. The Ultimate Spell.

The Ultimate Spell would help Ezmeralda take over the spiritual world making it all Dark-Sider and evil.

"Darla," I whispered, grabbing my bag off the desk. My bag lit up. I pulled Madame Torres out. The onyx ring that I had taken from Ezmeralda the last time we had met—the ring that gave her most of her power—floated inside of Madame Torres. It was in the top drawer of Colton's desk. I grabbed my bag and put it over my shoulder.

"Stop right there," Colton warned from behind me.

"Colton," I was never so glad to see a wand pointed at me. "Ezmeralda is back and she is trying to get my book. Trying to get the ring."

We both looked next to the desk. The yellow ball bounced up and down.

"June," Colton kept the wand pointed at me. "Get back in the cell and let me do my job. You've done enough damage for this village."

"You don't get it." I protested, "She's going to kill us all!"

"Get back in the cell." Colton started to walk closer.

The ball rolled under Colton's feet, causing him to trip over it. His wand skidded across the floor. I picked it up.

"I'm sorry, Colton." I opened the desk drawer and took the ring.

The ball bounced out the back and I followed with the ring and the Magical Cures Book in my hand.

The boy was helping me. I wasn't sure why, but I followed him and let him. The deeper we went into the woods, the further I moved into the world of the Dark-Siders. It was something I had never done, but knew I had to.

No doubt in my mind that Colton had already gotten to Oscar and told him what I had done.

"Help!" The voice off in the distance was Petunia. "Help!"

The ball darted ahead of me and I ran as fast as I could. The ball hovered in the air, showing me the way until I reached her. Petunia was surrounded by raccoons, squirrels and deer.

"June!" she yelled in a breathy voice. "Ezmeralda is here. She has put me in a fortress. My animals can't help me. She said she's here to take over."

The ostrich bolted forward. The ball bounced on its back.

"Paul Levy's spirit found the opening for the ostrich," Petunia said. "The boy and his father are united. Only the boy will always be a spirit with the ostrich. Neither will leave the other."

My mind was having a hard time wrapping around all of Petunia's words.

"You are right! I'm back!" A bolt of lightning came from the sky sending Ezmeralda down in front of me. "And I need those." She uncurled her long finger and curled it open and closed for me to give the ring and grimoire to her.

"Over my dead body," I said through gritted teeth and held the items close to my body.

"Oh, if you insist!" Ezmeralda brought her hand into the air. I closed my eyes, ready to take the blow.

"Mother! Stop!" Arabella rushed over to my side. "You will not do this."

My bag warmed against my body.

"I'm doing this for you. Us. Our family," Ezmeralda spat. Her words vicious to the ear.

"You are not my family." Arabella immediately disowning Ezmeralda caught her mother off guard.

"You have been poisoned. You will see once I get my ring and control the spiritual world." She lifted her hand.

"Stop!" Arabella walked up and stood between her mother and me. "I'll go with you. I'll help you if you let them go."

"No." I shook my head. "Don't you dare make a deal with her," I warned. "Let me take it for the world. I am the Chosen One."

"It would be a pleasure." Ezmeralda threw her head back and laughed.

The heat from my bag caused me to look. Madame Torres was glowing bright with a field full of Blood Mercy flowers.

My hand rose to my hair. I had forgotten I had stuck it in my hair for an accessory. I pulled it out, remembering the water and waves Madame Torres had shown me. With the flower pointed at Ezmeralda, I cracked the stem. Water flew out toward her.

"No!" Ezmeralda screamed in pain. "Not Blood Mercy! Arabella. . ." She reached for her daughter.

Arabella turned her head away from her mother as her mother's being disintegrated into a puddle of black tar before us.

CHAPTER TWENTY-FIVE

"Order! Order!" The Marys hammered their gavels on The Gathering Rock to get everyone's attention. "Order!" They yelled in unison. "Tell us exactly what you know, June."

Petunia, Gerald, and Eloise had all given their testimony to what they knew of Paul Levy. Now it was my turn to tell them exactly what had happened.

I walked in front of the Marys and took a deep breath. I could feel the love of my villagers behind me, giving me strength.

"It's simple really. Paul Levy's son died of a childhood illness. The death crippled Paul and he would do anything to get his son back. And selling his soul to Ezmeralda was his ticket. She was looking for a way to get back into Whispering Falls to get the ring and the Magical Cures Book with the Ultimate Spell. She made a deal with Paul—only Paul knew that he had to get in the bazaar by going through the village president. When he saw that Petunia wasn't sleeping, he offered her a deal any mother would take. Only baby Orin had to suffer through the mustache."

I glanced back at Petunia. As soon as Ezmeralda melted, the mustache disappeared from baby Orin, breaking the spell Paul had put on him.

"The ghost boy who almost ruined my wedding was here because he loved the ostrich. When Paul decided not to go through with the deed tasked to him by Ezmeralda after he saw my photo of Eloise in my shop, Ezmeralda followed him to the woods killing him and making it look like I did it." I pointed to Constance Karima. "The autopsy shows that Paul had a strike to the heart, which is Ezmeralda's specialty. One blow from her hand and you die."

The crowd behind me gasped.

"As Petunia told you, Ezmeralda confessed to coming back to take over the spiritual world. I had been named the Chosen One. I lived up to my title by killing Ezmeralda. Now I just want to be Oscar Park's wife and owner of A Charming Cure. Live a simple life in Whispering Falls." I smiled at Oscar.

He stood next to The Gathering Rock with his Whispering Falls police uniform on. There was pride on his face.

"I love you," he mouthed.

The Marys gathered in a circle, floating above the rock. They talked among themselves. I wasn't sure what their verdict would be and I wasn't sure what my punishment was going to be. All I knew was that I was Oscar's wife and I had fulfilled my destiny as the Chosen One.

The Marys floated down and landed square on their feet. Mary Ellen smacked the gavel on The Gathering Rock.

"Here by the Order of the Elders, we hereby sentence you to a week long honeymoon. Upon your arrival home, you will resume all duties as the owner of A Charming Cure and wifely duties to Sheriff Oscar Park."

The crowd behind me erupted in hoots and hollers. Oscar swept me off my feet and swung me around.

"I love you." I gave him little kisses all over his face.

"Honeymoon!" Oscar threw his head back and laughed. "Finally." He set me back on the ground. "Where are we going to go?"

"Somewhere sunny and not in the spiritual world." I grinned from ear-to-ear. I could already feel the warm sand between my toes.

The End

Keep reading for a sneak peek of the next book in the series. A Charming Hex is now available to purchase on Amazon or read for FREE in Kindle Unlimited.

BUT WAIT! Readers ask me how much my cozy mysteries and the characters in them reflect my real life. Well...here is a good story for you.

WHOOO HOOO!! I'm so glad we are a week out from last Coffee Chat with Tonya and happy to report the poison ivy is almost gone! But y'all we got more issues than Time magazine up in our family.

When y'all ask me if my real life ever creeps into books, well...grab your coffee because here is a prime example!

My sweet mom's birthday was over the weekend. Now, I'd already decided me and Rowena was going to stay there for a couple of extra days.

On her birthday, Sunday, Tracy and David were there too, and we were talking about what else...poison ivy! I was telling them how I can't stand not shaving my legs. Mom and Tracy told me they don't shave daily and I might've curled my nose a smidgen. And apparently it didn't go unnoticed.

I went inside the house to start cooking breakfast for everyone and mom went up to her room to get her bathing suit on and Tracy was with me. All the men were already outside on the porch.

The awfulest crash came from upstairs and my sister tore out of that kitchen like a bat out of hell and I kept flipping the bacon. My mom had fallen...shaving her legs!

Great. Now it's my fault.

Her wrist was a little stiff but she kept saying she was fine. We had a great day. We celebrated her birthday, swam, and had cake. When it came time for everyone to leave but me and Ro, I told mom that she should probably go get an x-ray because her wrist was a little swollen.

After a lot of coaxing, she agreed and I put my shoes on and told Tracy, David, and Eddy to go on home and we'd call them.

My mama looked me square in the face and said, "You're going with that top knot on your head?"

I said, "yes."

She sat back down in the chair and said, "I'm not going with you lookin' like that."

"Are you serious?" I asked.

"Yes. I'm dead serious. I'm not going with you looking like that. What if we see someone?" She was serious, y'all!

She protested against my hair!

Now...this is exactly like the southern mama's I write about! I looked at Eddy and he was laughing. Tracy and David were laughing and I said, "I can't wait until I tell my coffee chat people about this."

As you can see in the above photo, the before and after photo.

Yep...we went and she broke her wrist! Can you believe that? We were a tad bit shocked, and I'll probably be staying a few extra days (which will give us even more to talk about over coffee next week).

Oh...we didn't see anyone we knew so I could've worn my top knot!

As I'm writing this, you can bet your bottom dollar my hair is pulled up in my top knot!

Okay, so y'all might be asking why I'm putting this little story in the back of my book, well, that's a darn tootin' good question.

This is exactly what you can expect when you sign up for my newsletter. There's always something going on in my life that I have to chat with y'all about each Tuesday on Coffee Chat with Tonya. Go to Tonyakappes.com and click on subscribe in the upper right corner to join.

SNEAK PEEK OF A CHARMING HEX
BOOK 9

Chapter One

Ahh, the long and much needed sigh passed my lips. I lifted my chin up to the warm tropical sun and dug my toes in the hot, grainy sand. I'd never been to the beach. Darla never took me on a summer vacation. She said that the tourists ruined the natural habitats and she didn't want my images of Earth's natural beauty to be tainted at an early age, and that I had all my life to be influenced by outside forces she couldn't control when I became of age.

But I couldn't help but think that she'd love being here with me right now.

The crystal blue and almost white water was very calm. The small waves curled slightly over the sand, creeping up and hitting the tiptop of my toes. I smiled and glanced down the beach in both directions. No one was there. Just me and the white sand surrounding me as far as the eye could see.

"Oscar?" The flailing arms in the ocean caught my attention. Where was Oscar? "Oscar?" I pushed myself up to stand, not even worried about the hot sand that felt like a bed of hot rocks on the soles of my feet.

The arms went under and my instincts kicked in.

I dove into the vast ocean, surprised it was so deep as soon as I took my first step. Deeper and deeper I pushed myself, from the crystal blue into the suddenly-turning black, dark depths of the ocean with the arms of the man in sight.

A bright orange light pierced the darkness and dove in a spiral around the man. The man's body stiffened, his arms out to the side, his head thrown back, and his eyes looking over at me.

The water felt as if it turned to ice, my body was still warm, but the man's glare chilled the space between us. His eyes were diamonds. I watched as the spiral closed—he was gone. The spiral was gone. I pushed myself up toward the surface. The ice surrounded me. It sucked the air out of my lungs. I pushed harder, fighting the heaviness in my chest.

The light. The light of the bright sun pierced the surface of the water.

Just a little more. Push to the top. My mind told my body, but my arms were stuck to my sides as if there were concrete blocks tied to each finger. My shoulders moved rapidly back and forth. I kicked my legs. The light wasn't far, but the blackness engulfed me.

"Ahhh!" The animalistic sound escaped me from deep inside as I gasped for air.

"June." I heard the familiar voice and felt the strong hand stroke my back. "It's just a dream. Just a dream. Open your eyes. Please open your eyes."

When I tried to open my eyes, my inhale skipped down my nose and filled my lungs. The darkness filled with light as my body willed my eyes open.

"Oh, baby." Oscar pulled me into his safe and warm arms after my eyes found his face. His crystal blue eyes held concern. "It's okay," he assured me. He rubbed his strong hand down the back of my head as it rested against his chest.

"The beach." The words came out in a raspy voice as though my mouth was filled with the sand that I had just dreamed my toes were in. "There was a man drowning."

That was all I could remember. My nightmares were so intense, I swear my body and mind blocked the memories. One problem, I knew over the course of a few days, the memories would trickle back into my head and leave me with the memory of the full dream. And sometimes it was too late. I'd never had a nightmare where some part of it hadn't come true.

"You are just stressed," he assured me. "You've never been to the beach and you're not sure what to expect, but I promise," his heartbeat thundered in his chest; I pressed my ear closer to him, "I promise, we are going to have a wonderful time."

"I really think I need to take Mr. Prince Charming," I whispered and pulled away. I glanced around the room looking for my fairy-god cat.

"June," Oscar's head tilted. His hair was stuck up in different directions all over his head and as black as a raven's wing. "It's our honeymoon. Nothing is going to happen to us. I am a cop. I can protect us."

"But. . ." I gulped knowing that whenever I had a nightmare like the one I had just had, something evil was lurking.

"But nothing." He pulled the covers back and pushed himself up with his muscular arms and got out of bed. "I'm going to get in the shower. Don't be late for the council meeting."

I watched him disappear out the bedroom door. I waited until I heard the water turn on and the shower curtain pulled close before I reached over and rubbed the palm of my hand over the glass crystal ball of my other familiar, Madame Torres.

"Who is it that you seek? Or shall I say who seeks you?" The voice dripped out of the confines of the ball.

"I am open to who seeks me or the dangers surrounding my dreams." I could feel the fear in my voice as it trickled through my vocal cords.

I closed my eyes and let all the sounds and the feelings of the dream drift away from my soul. When I opened my eyes, Madame Torres had turned her ball into a clear calcite crystal. The small bubbles floated deep within her. My eyes focused on the center of her. The answer within the depth of Madame Torres told me everything I needed to know.

"Mr. Prince Charming," her voice was resigned.

Meow, meow. Mr. Prince Charming yawned. He was curled up in a tight ball at the foot of the bed.

My white, ornery fairy-god cat reached his front legs out in front of him, elongating his arms and spread his claws apart before his entire body waved in full stretch.

I tried to swallow the lump that had formed in my throat.

The clear calcite turned lavender and Madame Torres's face appeared, taking up most of the space within her ball. The orange turban perched on her head had a large diamond in the front where the material was gathered, bringing the memory of the man's eyes from my nightmare back into my head.

The waves deep in the ball moved like those of the ocean. Her eyes magnified, the bright yellow eye shadow covered her lids, bright red rogue was rubbed along her cheekbones, her lips stained ruby red.

"Mr. Prince Charming must accompany you and Oscar on your honeymoon." Madame Torres was well aware that Mr. Prince Charming was the last familiar Oscar wanted me to bring. Plus it wasn't easy trying to get a cat on a plane or to a tropical island. "Or you shall not go."

"So you do see some sort of danger?" I had to clarify. "We shouldn't go on the honeymoon?"

"What?" Oscar walked into the bedroom with a towel around his waist and another one in his hand dragging it through his wet hair. "We are going on a honeymoon. I'm taking you to the beach and we are going to be secluded. No one around but us. And no magic."

"Madame Torres said that. . ." I pointed to her but kept my eyes on his handsome physique.

"Madame Torres hasn't been outside of Whispering Falls and wants to go." Oscar sat on the bed and leaned toward my familiar.

The only thing he could see was her lavender liquid insides rolling around. He didn't have the gift of reading crystal balls. Oscar was a wizard and he only knew how to use his wand. But I could see the look on Madame Torres's face as she glared and then rolled her eyes in his direction. I smiled. Neither of my familiars got along well with my husband. I felt like I was constantly brokering peace between them.

"I'm going to head to Locust Grove and finish up my paperwork so we can be on the plane in the morning," he said in a stern voice. "Don't you think I'm a nervous wreck about flying? I've been to the beach a bunch but we always drove." He sat down on the edge of the bed next to me. "You are nervous about flying in a plane." He kissed my forehead. "It's really fun. I've flown several times and you are going to love it. Promise." He criss-crossed his heart with his finger.

Rowl. Mr. Prince Charming wasn't happy with Oscar's observation. He batted at us and darted off the bed.

I patted Madame Torres on the top of her ball when Oscar left the bedroom. I peeled the covers off me and got out of bed. There was so much to do before Oscar and I left and staying in bed worried about a nightmare that may or may not come true wasn't going to check the to-do items off my list.

I tooled around my cottage and got ready for the day while I waited for my coffee to brew. I loved where I lived. It was small and cozy. It had only one bedroom and bath along with the family room and a kitchen. But the view was undeniably the best feature. I leaned over the kitchen sink and stared out the window, overlooking the magical town I called home. Whispering Falls, Kentucky.

The morning sun was dripping over the mountains and spotlighting all the cozy shops that held secrets only the members of the village understood. Like Oscar, everyone who lived in Whispering Falls had a magical power. In mortal words we'd be called witches. In our world we considered ourselves Spiritualists.

My homeopathic cure shop, A Charming Cure, was my cover for my spiritual gift of potion making. It was a gift I had gotten from my spiritual side of the family—my father's side. I grew up in Locust Grove, a neighboring town about twenty minutes away, with non-spiritualist

Darla, my mother who didn't like to be referred to as Ms. Heal, Miss Heal, Mrs. Heal, or Mom. So I called her Darla. She was a mortal and tried to use my father's family journal to create homeopathic cures, but it wasn't until she died and I got my hands on the journal did the recipes come to life.

Growing up, Oscar and I lived next door to each other in Locust Grove and it wasn't until we were in our mid-twenties that Isadora Solstice came to Locust Grove and told us of our real heritage, along with introducing us to the magical village of Whispering Falls. It was here that we embraced our gifts and made it our home. Oscar was a police officer in both Locust Grove and Whispering Falls. It wasn't until a few months ago that we finally got married, but had yet to take a honeymoon.

It was easy for mortals to drop everything and go on a honeymoon, but it was different for us. Well. . .for me. My two familiars kept me safe from the outside forces and knew things before they happened. The nightmare for instance. I didn't have them a lot, but when I did, I had to be on high alert. I couldn't help but think I was having one because I was leaving the comforts of our small town like Oscar had said.

"I can't worry about the what if's," I said and poured myself a hot cup of coffee to go and made a mental note to grab some Mr. Sandman Sprinkles from my shop. Mr. Sandman was the best potion I had created to help me sleep. Though. . .I'd promised Oscar "no magic" on the honeymoon, but I was sure sanity trumped it.

Mewl, Mr. Prince Charming was perched on the back of the couch. He walked it like a tightrope and jumped off at the end. He stood at the front door. When I opened it, he darted out and down the hill toward Whispering Falls. His tail swayed back and forth. He was on a mission. I shook my head and locked the door behind me. He was like an old man in the village. Every morning he made his rounds to all the shops and greeted them.

Mr. Prince Charming had shown up on my porch in Locust Grove on my tenth birthday. I knew he wasn't a present from Darla. We didn't do birthday presents. We barely did cake. It was the only time Darla would let me eat sweets.

That particular year, the cake Darla had gotten me had *Happy Retirement Stu* written on it along with the manager's special sticker on it. Darla hadn't even bothered scrapping off Stu's name.

Mr. Prince Charming showed up with a dingy collar and a turtle charm that was missing an eye. Oscar gave me his mom's old bracelet for the charm. It was the best birthday I'd ever had.

I ran my hand over my wrist and felt my charm bracelet, bringing me out of my thoughts.

"See," I said out loud. "If I really were in danger, Mr. Prince Charming would've given me another charm."

I took a close look at all the charms he'd given me for protection. I was fine. I was safe. But I was still stressed and needed a June's Gem.

Just thinking about the chocolaty treat made my mouth water and I knew I had to make a pit stop at Wicked Good Bakery before I went to my shop. Without much more thought, I let my stomach and stress guide me and before I knew it, I was standing on the sidewalk right in front of Wicked Good Bakery.

Raven Mortimer was inside her bakery working away behind the counter and getting ready for the morning rush when Wicked Good opened. The green and pink awning above the shop windows flapped in the morning breeze.

Lightly I tapped on the door and got her attention. Raven's long black hair was pulled up in a ponytail; the Wicked Good apron was almost white from all the flour doused on it. She was rolling out dough, kneading it and shaping it when she looked up. A big grin scrolled up to her eyes. She rubbed her hands across the front of the apron before she walked over and unlocked the door.

"Get in here." She pushed the door open and hurried back behind the counter. "If I don't get these in the oven, I won't have a dang thing for my customers to purchase."

"Thank you for letting me borrow Faith. I know she does all your deliveries and works around here." Faith Mortimer was Raven's sister.

She worked for Raven part-time at the bakery, full-time as the editor-in-chief of the *Whispering Falls Gazette*, and part-time for me at A Charming Cure. Faith was going to work at the shop the entire time I was gone. "I'm so glad I don't have to close the shop for the honeymoon."

I gestured to one of the June's Gems she took out of the oven. It was her take on the Ding Dong and was named after me. She nodded.

"Are you getting excited?" she asked just as I took a bite of the savory cake.

"Mmm." I tilted my head side-to-side, my ears to my shoulders in a "meh" kind of way. After I swallowed, I said, "I had one of my nightmares last night."

"Really?" she asked and then scanned her eyes down her pastry counter. "I don't see anything here." She referred to her spiritual gift of Aleuromancy. She was able to see signs in her work, the dough. She made the most wonderful fortune cookies. She had a gift of putting in just the exact right fortune the customer needed.

"Good." I wiped across my mouth with the back of my hand. "That's a good thing."

"It sure is." Raven smiled and went back to kneading the ball of dough in front of her. "Faith is so excited to be in charge of the shop. She said she's going to redo the display window with a fun summer theme."

"That's what I love about her. She does whatever she wants." I pointed to another June's Gem. She nodded again.

"It's not like you to eat two, you must be stressed," she noted. "If I see anything before you leave, I'll be sure to let you know."

"Great." I grabbed one of the Wicked Good to-go bags and put the June's Gem in it. "This will make a great snack for before the meeting."

It was true. Ding Dongs were and are my stress-relieving treat. Raven invented the June's Gems and right now I was stressed out to the max.

"That's right!" She smacked the dough down on to the counter, flatting it out before she took the rolling pin doused in flour and flatted the dough more. "You find out from the village council where you get to go on your honeymoon."

"You know." I wagged my finger in the air and walked backward to the door. "Growing up as a mortal I had always envisioned my wedding. It was nothing like I had planned. Then I also had this idea in my head about my honeymoon." I shook my head. "I never imagined I'd be letting a group full of witches figure out where I was going to go." I referred to the council meeting today.

The village council had called a special meeting to decide where Oscar and I could go on our honeymoon. We were able to send in a list of destinations. Of course I wrote down Hawaii and Oscar wrote down Jamaica. Both of us wanted to go to a beach, that was for sure.

We were excited to find out which one they picked. Really either was good with me. Toes in the sand and a drink in my hand was how I was going to spend my much-needed week-long vacation.

"You're lucky." She wagged her brows up and down. She and everyone else in the village had been raised by their spiritual parents, unlike me and Oscar.

I gave a quick wave and out the door I went.

"June! Whoo hoo!" the voice called from down the sidewalk. It was Isadora Solstice. She stood at the steps of Mystic Lights. Her lighting shop was a cover up for her crystal ball reading spiritual gift. It was where I had found Madame Torres. Or rather Madame Torres finally found me.

Something else I'd had no idea about. The spiritualist didn't have a say in their crystal ball, the crystal ball picked the spiritualist. Madame Torres had sat on the shelf in Mystic Lights for centuries like a big round snow globe until I walked in. That was when she came to life and only I could see her.

"We moved the meeting time up so be there in an hour." She pushed her long blond wavy hair behind her shoulder before wiping her hands down her black A-frame skirt with the red hearts all over it. Her black pointy-toed boots were laced up tight. "I picked my skirt for you." She winked her big blue eyes and smiled. "For love." She clasped her hands as a delightful sigh escaped her.

"I'll see you soon!" I hurried across the street where A Charming Cure was located. I only had an hour to talk to Faith before the meeting and I wanted to make sure she was prepared, plus get my Mr. Sandman Sprinkles.

I stopped just shy of the gate that opened in front of the shop and looked down the street. Whispering Falls was so magical. The village was carved in the side of the mountain. The moss covered cottage shops were nestled into the woods and each had the most beautiful entrances. All the shops had colorful awnings with the shop's name on it.

The sidewalks on both sides were dotted with carriage lights with gas flames. Each shop had a special gate that led up to the shop steps, making the special village even cozier than it already was. There was already a line out the door of The Gathering Grove, the tea shop in the village. Tourists knew that they could go there for a nice breakfast before the rest of the shops opened.

A calmness came over me. I was being silly about going away. I was sure everything was going to be fine and Oscar was right. I was just stressed about my first time being on a plane and first time at the beach.

I opened the gate to A Charming Cure and a big whiff of the purple wisteria vine tunneled around me before I walked up the steps to the shop.

I reached up and ran my hand over the wooden sign that hung off the front of my cottage shop. The words *A Charming Cure* had replaced the *A Dose of Darla* sign after I moved here and accepted my spiritual gifts.

There were two shop windows and Faith was working in the right one. She was hanging beach balls from the ceiling. The ladder she was standing on teetered when I walked in.

"How on Earth did you get that?" I pointed to the four-foot tall sand castle made of real sand and reached to steady her.

"A little bit of magic." Faith's blue eyes sparkled. The teetering ladder didn't phase her. "Your honeymoon has inspired me. And I saw the new line of sunscreen you left in the back. Mortals love going on summer vacations and if they can get something from here, we need to jump on it."

"You are so smart." I took a moment to look at the shop. Tiered display tables dotted the shop's floor. Each table had a long red tablecloth that grazed the floor. Different sized and colored ornamental bottles sat displayed on each table.

When I had taken over the shop, I categorized the different potions for different ailments. I kept the big chalkboards that Darla had put on the wall with the daily specials. In fact, the chalkboard closest to the counter still had *A Dose of Darla* written on it in Darla's handwriting, something I couldn't erase.

Another thing I moved was the inventory. Darla had kept her inventory and ingredients in the back room. I had made a couple of open shelves behind the counter to display them. It was neat to see the different bottles and ingredients and made the shop feel more organic. I had turned the back room into a little sitting room and while I did put extra inventory in there, I mainly used it for a place to eat lunch or relax while working late.

Keeping the ingredients behind the counter was perfect for when a customer came in for something to help with what they thought ailed them, I would talk to them and immediately get a sense of what was really going on. My best seller was by far the antacids. Customers thought they had acid reflux or some other stomach ailment, when in fact the root of their issue was stress over money or heartache. It was then that I took the homeopathic bottle they had chosen from the sales floor and gave it a special touch to address what really ailed them. All of my customers returned because my homeopathic cures worked.

Sunscreen was going to be a big one this year along with all the weight loss potions. I had made one that helped with hunger, changed bad thoughts about body image, and boosted confidence. Faith was right. The quicker we sold it, the word would get out and we wouldn't be able to keep them in stock.

After Oscar and I had planned to go on a honeymoon and set the date, I knew I was going to need to make up potions for Faith to have on hand. I had stored them in the back room, leaving her with plenty of stock while I was gone.

"I have to go to the village council within the hour." On my way back to the counter, I tugged and smoothed my hands over the display tables' covers. It was very important to me to have a beautiful shop.

I stopped shy of the counter and looked at the framed photo of my parents, Darla and Otto Heal, hanging on the wall. They would've loved this shop. I knew they already loved Oscar because they showed up in Madame Torres while Mr. Prince Charming was walking me down the aisle. It was amazing.

My image reflected from the framed glass. My short black bobbed hair grazed my bare shoulders. My blunt bangs crossed my forehead in a perfect line. The white and blue striped bandeau top was new. I'd bought it from a shop in Locust Grove and paired it with white shorts and gladiator sandals. I was definitely ready for the beach.

"Are you okay?" Faith called out over her shoulder. A sand pail dangled from her long finger.

"I'm fine," I said and picked up the chalk for the chalkboard. "I need to write the daily specials." Quickly and in fancy cursive, I wrote the sunscreen specials on the board. "Tomorrow we can keep the same special, but change it to the weight loss special in a couple of days."

I took a step back and looked at the board. The smells of cinnamon, sage, dill and thyme swirled around my head. I smiled and took another look around.

I walked behind the counter to get a good look at the ingredients on the shelf, and nearly jumped of my skin when Mr. Prince Charming leaped up on the counter next to me.

Rowl. He barely opened his mouth. He dropped something and nudged it with his nose. I gulped after seeing the spiral-shaped charm he'd pushed toward me. Fear, stark and sheer ripped through me when the memory of the orange spiral from my nightmare jolted my insides.

"You don't look fine. In fact," Faith glided toward me, "you look worse than when I asked you."

I put my hand on the counter over the charm, hoping she didn't see it. I raked it into my palm and put it in my front pocket. There was no way I wasn't going on this honeymoon and there was no need to alarm anyone that Mr. Prince Charming had given me another charm.

"I'm fine." A nervous laugh escaped me. "I think I'm just nervous about leaving the shop and home."

"It's all good. I've got this." She pointed to herself, then at me. "You need to go enjoy that hunk of yours."

My mind wasn't wrapped around that hunk of mine; my mind was wrapped around the spiral charm. Mr. Prince Charming had been giving me protection charms since he showed up on my tenth birthday. The first one was a small turtle and anytime he felt I was in danger or going to be in danger, a new charm showed up.

I ran my hand over my wrist and curled my fingers around my charm bracelet. What if Mr. Prince Charming was trying to tell me something about my nightmares? Or what if Madame Torres was right about me having to take him with us?

I looked back at the shelf of ingredients and contemplated my options. I could make my Mr. Sandman Sprinkles and take them on my honeymoon just in case I needed it or just take my chances. My thought processes lasted all of a second, at the most, and I reached for the Aconite, the first ingredient for my potion.

I flipped on my cauldron and measured out 30 c of the Aconite, dumping it into the cauldron. I mixed in 6c Kali phos, 6c Nat suph, 3x passiflora and stirred it slowly. The liquid curled and bubbled, nearly flowing over the top of the hot cauldron. The frothy mix puffed a couple of smoke signals in the air. The smoke bubbles popped, sending the smell of fresh ocean salt air into the open space.

My cures took on the favorite smells of the person it was intended for making it even more appealing for the recipient. In this case, I was the patient of my own cure.

"You better get going," Faith called out and nodded to the clock on the wall. "You have to get up to The Gathering Rock."

The Gathering Rock was a communal space where we held our village rituals and village meetings. It was a sacred place. It was my job to smudge the area clean of any evil.

The Mr. Sandman Sprinkles rolled and roared inside the cauldron until it came to an abrupt stop. I ran my finger along the empty bottles on the shelf, knowing the bottle that was meant for this potion would glow as soon as my finger touched it. A small, white, milk glass bottle with a simple cork top lit up.

"Perfect," I whispered, grabbing the bottle. I took the cork off and held it over the cauldron allowing the potion to magically transfer from the cauldron to the bottle. It was a phenomenon that I didn't bother trying to explain or understand, it was just accepted like my spiritual gift.

The smudge ceremony bag caught my attention when I grabbed a rag under the counter to wipe the cauldron. Happily, I smacked my hands together. Faith jumped.

"I'm so sorry." I grabbed my smudge bag. All of my stuff for the trip needed to be smudged. I also grabbed a bottle with a generic potion in it. It would help me feel better and help keep me safe along with the charms. My intuition that I relied on was going to be on high alert. The generic potion would be good to take on my trip as a base to any potion I might really need to make.

"Wait." Faith stepped in front of me when I walked out from behind the counter with my Mr. Sandman Sprinkles bottle and smudge bag. "You aren't supposed to take any potions or witchy things on vacation. Orders of Officer Park."

"I'm going to take this to the meeting," I lied. If I told her the truth, she would've told Oscar I was smudging our house and luggage. I had promised him no potions, no spiritual stuff, just me and him on the honeymoon.

I couldn't help it if I had an obligation to my spiritual side. Even if I couldn't put it aside for a week.

Faith gave me the stink eye. She closed her eyes. She sucked in a deep breath in her nose and released it in a slow steady exhale out of her mouth. Her onyx eyes opened.

"I don't hear anything." She had tapped into her spiritual gift of Clairaudience.

"Or the fact that you just broke the law." I referred to one of the by-laws of the village. Spiritualists cannot read another spiritualist. The second by-law was that if you owned a shop in Whispering Falls, you had to live in Whispering Falls.

"Pish posh." She flailed a limp hand in the air before I grabbed my black cross-body bag and flung it across me. "Like no one else does."

She was right. Even though it was a law, it was unspoken that we did dabble in reading each other. Out of curiosity and protection of our kind.

"Now go." She pointed to the door.

Mr. Prince Charming jumped off the counter. His long white tail dragged along the floor as he waited patiently for me.

"And I don't want to see you in here again until you get back!" she shouted before I shut the door behind me.

I ran my hand down into my pocket and felt the charm. I looked down at Mr. Prince Charming.

"What on Earth does this mean?" I asked him, hoping he'd just open that little mouth of pointy teeth and tell me. He didn't. He darted down the steps, out the gate and between A Charming Cure and A Cleansing Spirit Spa.

"Hi-do, June," Chandra Shango waved from the stoop of her pink cottage shop's door. She owned the spa where she did nails, hair, and massages. She was a palm reader and the spa was the perfect cover. She gave out advice like candy to her clients. They loved her. She was always booked. "Are you getting excited to find out your honeymoon destination?"

"Wanna give me a hint?" I elbowed her as we met in between our shops. "Hawaii?" I did a hula dance to each side. "Or Jamaica Man?" I asked in my best Rastafarian accent, which was not too good mixed into my southern, hick accent.

She wagged her blue painted fingernails with the little gold star in my face. She had on a blue cloak with yellow stars all over it. Her yellow turban had a blue jewel in the middle to match the cloak. "You know I can't tell you, but you are going to love it. More relaxing then any old massage."

We talked about this and that on our way up the hill to The Gathering Rock. She told me about her new adventure in acupuncture. I wasn't sure I'd let her do that to me. I'd seen her go off track and I didn't want to be a pin cushion.

The Gathering Rock was exactly what it was named after, a big, gigantic rock that was in front of a clearing that served as a communal area. The village council already had chairs set up in front of the rock that was believed in the spiritual world to have powers in itself. Hovering over the rock with long black cloaks dangling down from the air, legs crossed and black hats pointing to the sky were the Order Of Elders. The Marys to be exact—Mary Lynn, Mary Ellen, and Mary Sue. They were retired village presidents of other spiritual communities and they only came around when there was a problem, like when I was accused of killing someone, which I didn't do.

My insides curled. I ran my hand over my pocket and felt the charm. Did they know what Mr. Prince Charming had given me?

"What are they doing here?" I whispered to Chandra.

"They are nosy." She tapped her nose. "Always got to be in everyone's business."

"Hi." Oscar walked over to us and bent down to kiss me. His lips were warm and soft. A calmness spread over me like wildfire. "I can't wait to get away with you." His eyes slid over to Mr. Prince Charming.

Mary Ellen had released her legs and floated down to the ground. She landed on her leopard-print boots. She bent down and picked up the ornery cat and stroked him. He purred so loud that you could hear him over the murmur of the council as they got ready to give us our honeymoon location.

Everyone's eyes were on me, and my intuition kicked in. My mind and body flooded with the spiritual rights of the smudging ceremony. I walked up to The Gathering Rock and took the smudging kit out of my bag. The sage stick was filled with cleansing ingredients such as sagebrush, sage, sweetgrass, lavender, cedar, mugwort, juniper, yerba santa, and rosemary, each used for a different purpose. Most of them were used for cleansing, clearing negative, encouraging awareness, purifying and healing. I was looking more to the cedar's component of deeply clearing negative emotions and replacing with positive energy to surround me and Oscar on our honeymoon to help negate the nightmares.

Once I lit the stick, everyone closed their eyes and bowed their heads. I walked around the circle of spiritualists and took a handful of the sage smoke and blew it toward each one of their hearts as I walked past each spiritualist. As each person took a deep breath to allow the healing smoke to fill their lungs, I waved the long feather to deepen their awareness of the healing power and whispered, "Breathe in positivity, courage and love."

The chants that came out of me were not something I had come up with. The chants would come out of my mouth on their own as I went deeper and deeper into my intuitive spiritual gift. This particular chant seemed to be appropriate since the council was here to give me and Oscar our destination.

"And now we call on our ancestors and all the animals of the spiritual world to carry our love and light to the rest of the world in order of protection, healing and love," my voice lifted into the air as I waved the smudge stick around in the middle of the group allowing the animals with wings to fly into the smoke and carry the messages from our spiritual world.

The feathered friends chirped and squawked before flying off into a deafening silence. Once the silence blanketed us, instinctively we all opened our eyes and moved to our rightful places in the council meeting area.

"Order! Order!" Petunia Shrubwood called, smacking the gavel a little too loudly for baby Orin who cried out from the kangaroo pouch hanging down her front. She was the Village President and all too happy to be in her position. She was an animal whisperer and owned Glorybee Pet Shop. She and Gerald Regiula were married and had baby Orin. "I'm so sorry baby boy," she whispered to Orin.

Gerald rushed over and grabbed Orin from the pouch to console him. He took the top hat off his head and fanned the baby. Orin loved the breeze and cooed with happiness.

The village council consisted of Gerald, Petunia, Isadora and Chandra.

"I'd like to welcome everyone to our special session today as we discuss the honeymoon destination for June Heal and Oscar Park." Petunia motioned for us to come in front of the council.

We stood next to each other holding hands. He squeezed mine and looked down at me. The love and compassion in his eyes always amazed me. It's hard to believe that I was married to my childhood best friend. He knew that Darla never gave me sweet treats and so would knock on my window in the middle of the night with a box of Ding Dongs. I knew then that I loved him. It wasn't until we were grown and living in Whispering Falls did we give in to our attraction and the chemistry between us.

"The Order Of Elders is here to reiterate that there must be no magic performed outside of Whispering Falls." Petunia looked back at the Elders. All of them nodded in agreement. "We know that Oscar understands, but we need to know from you, June Heal, that you understand the by-laws since it seems to be you that breaks them the most and gets herself in trouble."

My jaw dropped, my eyes lowered. I couldn't believe Petunia would say that to me. Nervously she looked away and bit her bottom lip.

"I get it," I said in a flat tone. "Ouch." I jerked my hand away from Oscar when he squeezed it a little too hard.

"Then we have picked your destination." Petunia nodded to Isadora.

"We've picked the small island in the Caribbean, Tulip Island." Petunia lifted the large crystal ball in the air, waving her hand over it.

"Tulip Island is a very small American island that only accommodates a few tourists at one time. This will help you keep a low profile and help stay out of trouble."

"Tulip Island?" Oscar stepped up. "I really wanted to go to Jamaica."

"I put down Hawaii." My confusion swirled around me.

"I'm sorry," Petunia couldn't even look at me. "Hawaii has the tiki legend and a spiritual community we'd like not to mingle with." She sucked in a deep breath through her nose. "And Jamaica has voodoo that we'd like to keep at a distance."

"It is certainly out of the question, with your wife's history, that we send you just anywhere in the world when we have to keep an eye on her." Elder Mary Sue pointed a finger at me. Her deep, brash voice boomed, "If you do not accept Tulip Island, you can honeymoon on top of the hill in your cottage."

"No, ma'am." Oscar stepped back in line. "We are more than happy to go to Tulip Island." He nudged me. "Right, honey?"

Mary Ellen put a squirming Mr. Prince Charming down on the ground. He ran over and reared up on his hind legs, batting his front paws on my pocket where I had put the charm.

"What is wrong with your familiar?" Elder Mary Lynn squeaked from the air. She stroked her fox stole that was around her neck.

"Oh no," Oscar groaned from under his breath.

A Charming Hex is now available to purchase or in Kindle Unlimited.

If you enjoyed reading this book as much as I enjoyed writing it then be sure to return to the Amazon page and leave a review.

Go to Tonyakappes.com for a full reading order of my novels and while there join my newsletter. You can also find links to Facebook, Instagram and Goodreads.

Join like-minded readers like YOU in the Cozy Krew Facebook Group for dream casting, fan theories, and live Q & A's. It's like a BIG GIANT BOOK CLUB! But if you want to have your own book club, be sure you let me know! I love to send goodies.

HAMMOCKS, HANDGUNS, & HEARSAY

Kenni Lowry Mystery Series
FIXIN' TO DIE
SOUTHERN FRIED
AX TO GRIND
SIX FEET UNDER
DEAD AS A DOORNAIL
TANGLED UP IN TINSEL
DIGGIN' UP DIRT
BLOWIN' UP A MURDER

Killer Coffee Mystery Series
SCENE OF THE GRIND
MOCHA AND MURDER
FRESHLY GROUND MURDER
COLD BLOODED BREW
DECAFFEINATED SCANDAL
A KILLER LATTE
HOLIDAY ROAST MORTEM
DEAD TO THE LAST DROP
A CHARMING BLEND NOVELLA (CROSSOVER WITH MAGICAL
CURES MYSTERY)
FROTHY FOUL PLAY
SPOONFUL OF MURDER
BARISTA BUMP-OFF
CAPPUCCINO CRIMINAL

Holiday Cozy Mystery
FOUR LEAF FELONY
MOTHER'S DAY MURDER
A HALLOWEEN HOMICIDE
NEW YEAR NUISANCE
CHOCOLATE BUNNY BETRAYAL

APRIL FOOL'S ALIBI
FATHER'S DAY MURDER
THANKSGIVING TREACHERY
SANTA CLAUSE SURPRISE

Mail Carrier Cozy Mystery
STAMPED OUT
ADDRESS FOR MURDER
ALL SHE WROTE
RETURN TO SENDER
FIRST CLASS KILLER
POST MORTEM
DEADLY DELIVERY
RED LETTER SLAY

Magical Cures Mystery Series
A CHARMING CRIME
A CHARMING CURE
A CHARMING POTION (novella)
A CHARMING WISH
A CHARMING SPELL
A CHARMING MAGIC
A CHARMING SECRET
A CHARMING CHRISTMAS (novella)
A CHARMING FATALITY
A CHARMING DEATH (novella)
A CHARMING GHOST
A CHARMING HEX
A CHARMING VOODOO
A CHARMING CORPSE
A CHARMING MISFORTUNE
A CHARMING BLEND (CROSSOVER WITH A KILLER COFFEE COZY)
A CHARMING DECEPTION

A Southern Magical Bakery Cozy Mystery Serial
A SOUTHERN MAGICAL BAKERY

A Ghostly Southern Mystery Series
A GHOSTLY UNDERTAKING
A GHOSTLY GRAVE
A GHOSTLY DEMISE
A GHOSTLY MURDER
A GHOSTLY REUNION
A GHOSTLY MORTALITY
A GHOSTLY SECRET
A GHOSTLY SUSPECT

A Southern Cake Baker Series
(WRITTEN UNDER MAYEE BELL)
CAKE AND PUNISHMENT
BATTER OFF DEAD

Spies and Spells Mystery Series
SPIES AND SPELLS
BETTING OFF DEAD
GET WITCH or DIE TRYING

A Laurel London Mystery Series
CHECKERED CRIME
CHECKERED PAST
CHECKERED THIEF

A Divorced Diva Beading Mystery Series
A BEAD OF DOUBT SHORT STORY
STRUNG OUT TO DIE
CRIMPED TO DEATH

Olivia Davis Paranormal Mystery Series

About Tonya

Tonya has written over 100 novels, all of which have graced numerous bestseller lists, including the USA Today. *Best known for stories charged with emotion and humor and filled with flawed characters, her novels have garnered reader praise and glowing critical reviews. She lives with her husband and a very spoiled rescue cat named Ro. Tonya grew up in the small southern Kentucky town of Nicholasville. Now that her four boys are grown men, Tonya writes full-time in her camper she calls her SHAMPER (she-camper).*

Learn more about her be sure to check out her website tonyakappes.com. Find her on Facebook, Twitter, BookBub, and Instagram

Sign up to receive her newsletter, where you'll get free books, exclusive bonus content, and news of her releases and sales.

If you liked this book, please take a few minutes to leave a review now! Authors (Tonya included) really appreciate this, and it helps draw more readers to books they might like. Thanks!

Cover artist: Mariah Sinclair: The Cover Vault

Made in the USA
Las Vegas, NV
04 May 2023